Dancing in the Dust

Dancing in the Dust

A novel

Kagiso Lesego Molope

We acknowledge the support of the Canada Council for the Arts for our publishing program. We also acknowledge support from the Ontario Arts Council.

Cover photo by Peter Magubane, courtesy UN Photo Library, Department of Public Information, United Nations.

National Library of Canada Cataloguing in Publication

Molope, Kagiso Lesego, 1976-
    Dancing in the dust / Kagiso Lesego Molope.

ISBN 1-894770-01-3

    I. Title.

PS8576.O45165D36 2002   C813'.6   C2002-905470-2
PR9199.4.M64D36 2002

Printed in Canada by Coach House Printing

TSAR Publications
P. O. Box 6996, Station A
Toronto, Ontario M5W 1X7
Canada

www.tsarbooks.com

Written in honour of my father's spirit

Setshwaneng W. Molope

It was not restraint I had to learn, but ways to use my rage to fuel actions, actions that could alter the very circumstances of oppression feeding my rage.

AUDRE LORDE, *A burst of Light*

If you're watching, you can see them laughing and playing in their innocence. This street is all they know. Don't think for a second that they don't try to imagine what may exist a hundred, or a hundred thousand, kilometres from here, because it is all they ever do: imagine, dream, imagine, dream. There are futures in their fantasies, places they will go to when they grow up and leave, places with smells and colours they know well because they've been there so many times in their imaginations. For now, because there are no choices, they live and love and play and trust only in this street. They trust its grooves shaped by the rains, its dust, and its little rocks. They trust the street because you trust what is most familiar. Of course, this very street will turn and swallow them whole one day. That is what it was designed for. Only a few of them will be left, clinging for dear life. Those who can get away will, and may they never look back—God help them!

Many thousands of kilometres away, those who have lost all trust in their streets—small nations (who reflect a great majority) in cold, remote parts of the world—have sent out a plea for help, begging the world to take and save what is left of these children.

1

IN MY BACKYARD the peach trees had shed most of their fruit, and the few peaches that still clung to the branches were rotting in the heat. We were in typical post-thunderstorm conditions; the hail had beaten down on the trees and left them looking almost as they do in winter. From a distance I tried to find a single peach that looked edible, but I wouldn't go close to the tree or walk around it for fear of squashing the fruit and making a sweet puddle on the ground. This was one of those lazy, overheated afternoons where even we children could not brave the streets for too long, so for entertainment I was sitting alone, letting my mind play games with the peach trees. Although it didn't feel like one of those dangerous afternoons we were constantly anticipating, the kind where policemen in their obnoxious and invasive green vans roamed the streets to make us feel uncomfortable in our own territory and then left with a few victims, the quiet of the neighbourhood was making me nervous. I had to keep my mind on something easier to contemplate. Serenity around here had become so unfamiliar that when it did come it made you suspicious. The place was always noisy since, at any given point, there were weddings, parties, street fights, street games, or riots. Silence was chilling. It had you thinking that whatever was happening a few streets over—that very thing that had drawn people away from here—was surely on its way. You felt the need to brace yourself, because it could be death or celebration, and since both were constant visitors you could never guess ahead of time.

So I was only a little bit relaxed as I lay there, with half my body in the sun and the other half in the shade of the house's brick wall, constantly alternating the two. Head in the sun for five minutes, then feet in the sun for the next five to fifteen minutes—the feet could stand it longer than the eyes could. This was my attempt at absorbing as much sun as I could manage, something I did because I was trying to get darker, having grown weary of my light skin, which stuck out like a sore thumb in my township. If it had just been the neighbours who looked totally different from me, I probably would have felt less awkward. But even in my house everyone looked more like each other than they looked like me. Of course, people would comment on my difference, which only made me more curious, so that I kept asking my mother a million questions. But as I was getting older I learned not to ask the questions I had asked before with the innocence of a child, because Mama forbade me from ever questioning what seemed to set me apart from everyone, including my family. I had come to understand that asking questions like that was seen as a suggestion that there were embarrassing secrets in my family, and this offended Mama so deeply that it made me feel ashamed of myself. So I had almost learnt to accept that not all siblings looked exactly alike, despite seeing that no one looked less like a member of their own family than I did. But it was a subject I constantly dwelt on, especially at times when I found myself alone, as on this particular afternoon. After a while the questions I was itching to ask never made their way to my lips and so never had a voice. But they stayed in my mind and occasionally they would travel to my head and limbs, so that I would be temporarily paralyzed by some of the explanations I came up with on my own.

"Tihelo, don't you have anything to keep you busy?" Mama startled me. Head in the sun, I looked up and shielded my eyes with my hand so I could see her better.

"I already cleaned the kitchen," I said in my weak defence.

"Then clean your messy room."

"I cleaned my room this morning," I protested.

My mother hated being argued with, and of course I knew that cleaning my room or the kitchen was not the point. The problem was that she hated seeing me play this game in the sun. She would find anything for me to do if it meant getting me out of the sun and seeing me use my hands. She rested both fists on her hips, and I got nervous. Fists on the hips were a definite sign of my mother's growing impatience.

"There is *ting* sitting in the cupboard, and I know it won't ferment itself."

I had lost my defence, and my balance from the heat, so, giving up on the possibility of a good peach, I stood up, steadied myself, and headed for the kitchen to ferment the sour porridge. But I was still feeling uneasy about the silence in the neighbourhood. I thought it seemed impossible that everyone might have gone indoors to sleep or sit, this kind of heat did not let you do either. People were usually either sitting under large trees while they did some kind of work with their hands, like sisters platting each other's hair, old women knitting scarves and table mats to sell later, or families working together in their gardens. The thought of a person just sitting and doing nothing was so repulsive to people that even as a grown woman I still feel guilty when I find myself with no work in my hands. I can almost always find something to do.

I was going to put the bag of *ting* back in the cupboard when the silence broke, and rather abruptly. There were sudden screams and cheers that pulled me to the front of the house. Then I saw Mohau, a schoolmate who lived across the street from us, running with a crate full of milk cartons, and his brother Tshepo running right behind him carrying about six cartons of milk in his arms. Everyone was out of their houses, either standing at their gates or yelling at their children to hurry up and get themselves some milk. I asked around and a neighbour explained that a milk truck had been stopped and hijacked on the main road—the only paved road—by a group of comrades in the name of freedom fighting. Within seconds there was everyone I knew, and strangers too, moving like lightning towards where the milk truck was supposed to have been, the possibility of over a week's supply of food looming in the road ahead. I was excited but did not dare follow the crowd because I knew what Mama would have to say about us picking up food from the road. I watched enviously until I started wondering about the expiry dates on the cartons, and how much milk each family could go through in a day.

The street had come alive and felt more familiar. I stood marvelling at the exhilarating exercise of fighting for freedom, watching women and men running around yelling "take back what belongs to the people." But just as I was completely absorbed in the mayhem, Mama yelled out to me from her bedroom window, telling me to come inside.

"There'll be police vans around here in no time. Everyone should stay inside," she warned those within earshot.

I panicked as I always did at the mention of police and decided to watch it all from inside the house. What I did not know was that there would not be much to see because, as Mama had predicted, our street was infested with green vans in less than an hour. But at that point the "dogs," as the police were known, had neither culprits nor witnesses to attack. I was amazed at how quickly the word "police" could make people's feet move. Just the image of a policeman brought so much fear in us that we would drop whatever we were doing and disappear within seconds. It was not surprising, then, that the police eventually arrived fully armed as hunters always do, with their dark green uniforms looking as terrifying as ever. They walked and drove around foolishly for an hour and then eventually went away from what had become a completely silent and deserted street. The world was quiet and eerie again. I imagined that everyone was holding their breath just as I was doing, and so none of us made a sound.

That night I lay awake on my bed replaying the events of the day over and over in my head, fascinated mostly by the speed with which people had moved. In my mind I had stopped the truck along with the other comrades, and I had been the first to come to our street with a crate of milk. All the women, including Mama, had been running beside me with their crates. Everyone had followed the tracks of my shoes, going where I had gone first. I grinned at the pictures in my mind until sleep crept in.

2

MAMA IS AN exceptionally tall woman. She may like it or she may not. It just isn't important to her to spend any amount of valuable time—and it's all valuable to her—talking about how she looks. However, in my early teens I began noticing changes in my body, which meant that I had also been paying attention to the shape of women around me, especially my mother's. I had always been aware of how different I looked, how I was a lot lighter-skinned than most people I was growing up around. I obsessed over my colour, but that was nothing out of the ordinary because the entire country and its laws were based on obsessing over your colour. At the time I saw a lot of sense in that fixation, even if it often made me feel uncomfortable. But thinking about how my body was built was different because I marvelled over it. I enjoyed how everything had begun to take on its own shape and stretch in its own direction. My breasts were round and hard, my backside was growing bigger and higher, and my limbs were stretching away freely. My thoughts were telling me that my body was beginning to reflect my mother's and my sister's, and that definitely was part of the excitement. I watched my mother a lot and imagined myself being the spitting image of her when I reached my thirties, or whatever age she was.

My mother's name is Kgomotso, which means "to comfort," a name she got because she was born after a brother who died young of an unknown illness. This was according to family talk, but I've heard enough talk to know that "unknown" meant "not to be disclosed to the children." She was like every other mother I knew: she worked all of her days, had a good idea about everything and everyone around her, and almost never cried. Parents never cry, except at funerals and sometimes even at weddings. My sister's name is Keitumetse, which means "I am happy." The story was that there had not really been that much joy when she was born because Mama was supposed to finish nursing school first and *then* have a baby. Having a baby instead meant that she gave up nursing school and was now working in the kitchens. She was gone from about an hour before dawn to about an hour after dusk, seven days a week, leaving my sister and me to take care of ourselves when we woke up in the mornings and when we came home from school in the evenings. She had to make sure she caught the five-thirty train into town in order to arrive at work on time. She must have known that having a baby would leave her no choices. But even so, I think it took a lot of courage to give an unwelcome child that name. Most people usually give their unplanned children names that are apologetic, like "forgiveness," "mercy," or "be welcoming." However, anyone who knew my mother well would never expect her to apologize for something that belonged to her.

I got the bit about the unplanned pregnancy from my sister, who had perfected the art of sitting under tables on lazy afternoons, playing and pretending to be deaf, while the adults disclosed the secrets of their anger. On her good days my sister would tell me everything I was never supposed to know, like how our father was swallowed by the City of Gold, or Gauteng, right after I was born, and how the story about him dying from heart disease was a fabrication meant to sustain our respect for him. Many men had disappeared into the gold mines throughout the years, so this didn't come as a shock to me. It was the lying that baffled me. I mean, I did not feel that was a necessary strategy since I was not one to get caught up in thoughts about someone I had never known. I never missed him so they may as well have been truthful with me. At that age I had not begun to grow curious about him since the truth of my own history had not yet been disclosed to me.

All I thought was that it was sad how everyone assumed that I needed this person just because some other children had someone like him in their lives. Personally, I had no complaints about being raised in a home run by women, but because of my age no one ever asked my opinion. There is always the belief that a house with no men is missing something essential. Men were always asking us if we needed help fixing things, and boys we played with voluntarily took on the role of older brothers to me and my sister because they thought we needed extra protection. I got the sense that people saw us the way you see someone who is missing a limb: you assume their entire lives are really sad and inadequate just because you can't imagine your own life being full were you in the same position. And you never bother to find out if you're right so you go on assuming it and never seeing the other person as whole. In the same way, no one ever got to fully understand that my family felt to me as full and whole as anyone else's. My mother wanted me and my sister to respect and honour the memory of our father, but she never asked our forgiveness for not bringing us someone to replace him. Even after all the events that took place in my adult years, my mother and my sister remain the only family I have ever known, the only two people I have ever longed for when I was desperate for the comfort of family.

Of course, there were other people who were always there looking and watching. We were a community of people brought together by circumstances meant to destroy us, so we watched over each other. Mohau had a grandfather who sat every day on a chair under a tree that was right in the front of their yard. He would tell you every single person he saw go in and out of your house if you were out during the day. My mother trusted him so much there was never any worry about our house being broken into. And we too, the children of that street, took comfort in knowing that he was watching our every move. When Mohau broke into a fight over a bicycle with Thabo, another friend and neighbour, they were at the east end of the street, but his grandfather knew very well who had started it because he had been observing them long enough and because none of us were ever too far away for him to see. All parents were everyone's parents to a certain extent. If my friend Thato's mother wanted someone to go to the store for her and Thato was not around, I would be expected to go instead. If Mohau was sick and needed to go to the hospital, Thato's mother would be expected to take him because she had a car and Mohau's mother did not live with him. It went on like that for years and I have respected and trusted all of these older and elderly neighbours all my life.

Then there was Mma Kleintjie. She was Coloured, which meant she had White ancestry or was a descendant of the people of the bush. Either way, she held a slightly different and better status in the country because of her lighter skin colour, her green eyes, and the texture of her hair. How she had come to live in a Black township was a mystery to us all, since she hardly talked to anyone. Only adults knew her well, but even they did not know why she lived there and why she had never lived with anyone but herself. All the children feared her because of her mysterious nature and the fact that she was always watching us play, but she would never ever talk to us. Mma Kleintjie—her Afrikaans name confirmed that she was Coloured and not Black—was even scarier because, even though she watched us like a hawk, she really and truly seemed to hate children. We were never out of her sight, but she was not looking with the warm and caring eyes that we saw in the rest of the adults. We all feared her. If we accidentally threw a ball in her yard while playing, none of us would go in there to fetch it. I remember spending an entire afternoon playing only the games you could play with rocks because someone had kicked our ball so far that it landed near her *stoep*. Children told stories of how she was really a witch and how she had slaves under her bed who could not speak—*ditloutlwane*, what everyone called little slaves. They were supposed to have been people whose families thought were dead but who were actually living under someone else's roof, their spirits possessed by the owner of the house. Mma Kleintjie, like other witches, had supposedly taken them and cut out their tongues so they would never speak, and turned them into her personal slaves.

For me, what made Mma Kleintjie even stranger was that Mama always warned me to never ever listen to anything she said. Since this woman never spoke I didn't understand what that was about, but it made me curious about her. I wanted to hear her voice, to know her thoughts and how her mind worked. Although my mother never gave any explanation of why I was to stay away from her, I always sensed that it was along the same lines as being told to never speak to strange men in cars with dark windows. It was a warning I never took lightly, and I knew it should be one of the last things I went against. But my curiosity about her was gnawing at me, the same way I wondered about what exactly the man in the dark-windowed car did with children who spoke to him. I was interested but equally terrified. So I kept engaging in conversations about Mma Kleintjie. It was very interesting to hear what children on my street thought they knew about her. Sometimes I went to Ausi Martha, a neighbour whose house I had spent many years of my childhood in because she watched me when my mother went to work. I usually could get any answer from her, even the ones children were not supposed to know, like why someone had stopped working or why a man did not live at his home any more. But she never answered my questions about Mma Kleintjie. Whenever I brought up the Coloured woman's name, it was as if I had said a bad word. Ausi Martha would look really angry with me and tell me to stay away from *Lekhalate*, the Coloured person, as we all called Mma Kleintjie. Eventually my curiosity wore off and I tired of wondering about her. I stopped asking questions, until the first time I came face to face with her.

*

When I was seven years old, I cut the bottom of my foot from stepping on broken glass while playing rounders, a street game almost similar to baseball but played with a tennis ball that you throw rather than bat. I hopped home in a panic, screaming "Mama! Mamaaaa!" My mother carried me in her arms and took me to the water tap, which was outside in the wall near the kitchen window. She soaked my foot in a bowl of water and antiseptic liquid; the wound stung as soon as I put my foot in the mixture. To calm me, my mother rubbed my chest with her palm. Having my chest rubbed, a gesture of compassion, had always comforted me.

But I was startled that day when I saw my mother cry, one of only two times I had seen her in tears. I immediately assumed that it was because I was crying and so I stared up at her apologetically. She sat me down and dressed my wound and told me this: "There is nothing for us here. What we live is not a life . . . so many people I know are gone now, all of them either lost or killed. Neither one is better than the other, and don't fool yourself, there isn't a place in this country that was designed for your survival." Two of her high-school friends who had disappeared months before had been found dead in a prison in Pretoria. The police ruled it a suicide and thought it unnecessary to continue with an investigation. Mama told me about the two men, expressing how much she loved the time she had spent with them. She spoke in that way that we all speak of people we miss and who we know we will never see again, with nostalgia embedded in love, and with an exaggeration of the dead persons' goodness. She was mourning and I was not too young to understand that it was probably one of her most painful experiences. It was all too much for me and I sought her comfort, but as an adult I've come to realize that although what my mother and I were feeling may have been different at the time, we were probably equally overwhelmed.

3

THATO MOROKA WAS my closest friend. She lived three doors away from me, and her house looked a hundred times different than ours. The government had built us homes that resembled each other, with every second house facing the same way. One house faced the road, and then the next faced sideways. All of these houses had four rooms, and that is what they were called: "four-rooms." The only thing that set them apart was their colour—either red, white, orange, or green. The doors were positioned a little high, so that you had to watch your step every time you walked out of your house, but people had taken care of that by building their own *stoeps*. In fact, people had taken care of a lot of things to make these houses more livable. Those who could had bought bathtubs for their bathrooms so that they would no longer have to bathe in the same small round buckets they used for washing their clothes. And if you could eventually manage to buy your house from the government of the homeland you were living in, you could even paint the outside, install large windows, and pave the yard so you wouldn't be faced with blinding dust in August. We were redesigning our homes to make them look and feel like we had a hand and a choice in how we lived.

Then there was the "six-room." Almost always at the corner of a street, the six-room was the one with three bedrooms instead of two. It was shaped very differently, had a porch in front of the kitchen, and was just *large* in our eyes. Not surprisingly, the occupants of the six-rooms were almost always people who earned more money than the rest of those around them. They would be teachers or nurses or school principals. Or they would have a small business in the township, like a liquor store or a grocery store.

Up the hill was a handful of houses that were occupied by professionals and store owners whose businesses were doing well enough that they could build their own houses. Another paved road was being built that was soon to separate the masses from the people on the hill. Although where we lived was officially known as the township, we also called it all kinds of different things that really meant nothing, such as *lekeishene* (the location), reservation, and *kasie* (also location or place).

This was Thato's reality: she lived in a six room, and her parents each had their own car. Her mother was a nurse and her father owned a small grocery store. She was the first child in the township to get a BMX, and roller skates, and before that every toy that the rest of us could only dream of.

She was my favourite person in the world apart from my family, which was fine because I was her favourite person in the world too. I was also her favourite storyteller. Friday afternoons after school—because then we had the entire weekend to do schoolwork—we would sit on the ground in the sun and play with little rocks, telling stories based on things both imagined and overheard around us. They would often go like this:

Father rock: *Woman, you talk too much, I'm going to get myself some beer.*

Mother rock: *What will people say about me? You embarrass me! You're always drinking!*

Father rock slams the door behind him and stomps off to the Shebeen. Mother rock runs after him and stands at the gate yelling: *I'll find myself another man! Don't come back into my house, I'm marrying another man!*

We would go on and on entertaining each other. We would have the mother and father rocks kissing, having sex, and doing all kinds of things we were not supposed to be caught talking about. Mostly the kinds of things you would hear about while sitting with the older youths, the high-school students. We had gone to the same primary school and we were now just reaching the end of our three years together at our middle school. I never went a day without seeing Thato. We shared everything from my gossip and wit to her luxuries. There was nothing she knew that I didn't, and we intended to always have it that way. Some days in school she would bring me sweets and chocolate bars from her father's store or from her kitchen cupboard just after her parents had filled it up with goodies. They were a treat not only because I loved chocolate, but also because my mother never spent much money on chocolates—she just didn't believe in spoiling our teeth, and she could not afford to spend money on things we didn't need. I loved going to Thato's house for these reasons: Thato's parents could fill their house with things that you only bought because you wanted to, not because you needed to. There was the study, a room filled with books going up to the ceiling. Then, of course, the fancy living room sofas, the garden chairs you could lie on and bask in the sun, and the soap dish and perfume in the bathroom. I loved it. I would have my mind going all sorts of places whenever I was in there. I imagined I was somewhere far, far away from the *lekeishene*, meeting people, changing the world, being important.

The Morokas were also the first people to have a television and every child on the street would go to their house to watch shows like *The A-Team*, which was on before the news at seven o'clock on Thursday nights. We would watch and then leave when the music for the news came on. The *A-Team* was in English on TV1, the English and Afrikaans channel, and despite how little we understood of the American speech, we all remained hooked. The older youths understood more because they had to read more complicated English books in high school—the language was not so confusing to them at that point. The rest of us were just excited by the action on the small screen. It was one of the only times we watched TV1, because we lived in a Sesotho-speaking township and mostly watched TV3, which aired in Sesotho, Sepedi, and Setswana.

TV2 had the Nguni languages like Sezulu, Sexhosa, Setsonga, and Sevenda. We hardly ever turned on TV2 because most of us understood very little of it. None of us were learning it in school because we were in a designated Setswana enclosure. However, Afrikaans and English were both mandatory, even if all of us could speak Afrikaans better than English since we began learning it first in Grade 1. English was a lot more complicated and harder to comprehend, even for most adults, since those who had gone to school had been taught every class in Afrikaans and people who worked in town were working in Afrikaans. Hardly anyone could say they did not understand a little bit of the Dutch-like language.

My life felt perfect around Thato. Karabo was another girl exactly our age that we often played with, but neither Thato nor I were as close with her as we were with each other. All of us played together with Thabo, Peter and Tshepo, and all the other children on our street but we liked each other best of all. My sister and Mohau would also play, but something had been happening to Keitumetse that made her like our company less and start enjoying the sight of her face more and more. She spent more time in front of the mirror than she did on the streets, and the same went for Mohau.

Even though I missed her, I was happy enough to have Thato that it only made a difference when my friend was away on holiday. Things were perfect. I still maintain that a child's innocence—although it can be their worst enemy—is often their best protection. Although the constant rioting was disturbing, I knew and understood very little about what exactly was going on in the law and so I played and loved and laughed carelessly in those years. We all did. I remember caring so little about the year ahead of us, loving every hot day—especially being convinced I was definitely getting a little darker.

But it was around that same time that my anxiety was to increase and some unsettling changes began to take place all around me. It was my last year of middle school, the year my street joined in a project that was going on around every township, where everyone was taking care of their street, cleaning it and growing gardens at each street corner. I got very involved in this because I really liked the idea of building ourselves "parks," as we called the small gardens and it was bringing out everyone's creative energy. Tshepo was painting a mural on the "stop nonsense", a wall-like high fence that people only put around their yards if they didn't get along with their neighbours. The rest of us were divided between taking out the weeds, planting flowers and grass, and bringing rocks that we were going to paint and use as chairs to sit on. Some people were carving wood to make a figure that was supposed to be an imprisoned African National Congress, or ANC, member wearing a T-shirt that said "Release Our Leaders." It was a sign in support of all political prisoners. It was invigorating working on a project together, building something that was going to be all ours. There was no parental supervision because some of the people working in the park were in high school and they knew what they were doing, so they were to handle sharp instruments, make rules and watch us the younger ones.

We must have spent about a week putting our park together. There were many of us working at it since every child from every house had come out to help, and so we covered a lot in very little time. For days after we had been working we would just walk past there to admire our work and every morning someone would go and water the plants and the lawn. Our park was growing, almost looking like something you would see when you went into town, something that would have a sign meant to keep you from getting close and enjoying the green space. This one was ours. After it was built we forgot that it was a space we had created to sit in, we enjoyed it from a distance. We admired and protected it so much that you would never see anyone actually sitting there on the painted rocks—no one wanted to step on the grass and ruin it. On every street, if there was enough space around the corner house, people built themselves a park and never played in it. Eventually it was like a competition: Whose park was the cleanest? Who had the best designs? We once saw one with flowers and paintings so perfect that we never went around that corner very much any more because we wanted to believe it couldn't get better than ours.

Living in the townships involved the blindest and most fierce kind of faith—you could believe in an invisible and all-powerful force, but your best bet was probably to have that unrelenting self-confidence and in one's neighbours. Although this was a world we were thrown into forcefully and without choice, we were often working at making it feel more and more like a place we could justify calling home.

One morning as I was watering the lawn, I sat with Tshepo talking about his mural and all the other drawings he had done. He had a small notebook where he had a collection of his work that he showed me. I admired his talent and he enjoyed telling me stories behind the sketches. He described many of his creative processes, such as spending an evening painting an image of Jesus surrounded by children on the wall of the church his family went to. It was something he had done because the priest had offered him money for it. Eventually I was tired of hearing about him, so I suggested we go and play another game. But he was not interested in a game, he was only anxious to reveal something to me.

"Do you know how to make a petrol bomb?" he said out of the blue.

I said, "No, and neither do you." He could create stories as well as he could draw, so I knew he was about to lie and show off.

"I know how because my brother told me. Remember the milk truck he hijacked?"

As soon as he said "my brother" I knew it was another one of his "my brother the hero" stories and I was already losing interest. Tshepo had such high admiration for his brother; he made it look like the single most important person to have in one's life was an older male sibling—which of course had me feeling annoyed and sometimes even defensive. At those times I was all ready to tell six different stories about the greatness of my sister. But he had put his notebooks down on a red rock next to him and gotten closer to me so it was beginning to look like he had quite a story coming.

"He didn't hijack the milk truck, he was on his way home when he saw that happening. He just picked up a crate and ran home," I said.

"*Ja! Ja!* He hijacked it—him and my aunts! I saw them, I was there!"

"So? The truck wasn't bombed, why are you asking about bombs?"

"No," he began, his voice dropping too a whisper. "But the people they were with—the comrades—they know and they've been making them for years. They were teaching my brother because he is one of them now. He's a comrade," Tshepo whispered the revelation and then added, "but my parents don't know."

"Even your grandfather doesn't know?" I said this raising my voice and meaning it more as an expression of shock than a question.

"No, no one in my house knows except for me. My aunts don't even know that I know. My brother said I shouldn't tell them because they think I'm too young."

I began pulling out something that looked like weeds growing around some flowers. I was feeling annoyed because I believed him, it was clear this was not going to be one of his made up stories about what he knew. It made me both jealous and somewhat nervous that Tshepo had a skill so intriguing and dangerous. I would have thought none of us would ever possess such power.

"So," he continued despite my attempts at showing no interest. "Do you want me to show you how?"

I shrugged and he took it as enthusiasm. We walked around for a minute and picked up a beer bottle that had been thrown in the middle of the street along with everything else that belonged in a rubbish bin.

Tshepo took the bottle and half filled it with some soil. We went around again for about a minute or two looking for a piece of cloth, which he stuffed in the bottle so that a little bit of cloth was sticking out.

"We don't have petrol now, but what you do is pour in half before you put the cloth in, then you light up the end of the cloth that's sticking out, shake the bottle really quickly and then throw!"

I was fascinated and afraid at the same time. I thought, anyone who can do that can hold so much power in their hands—petrol bombs have brought down whole buildings.

"That's what we used to burn the post-office two weeks ago," Tshepo said in a whisper.

"You?"

"Yes, me and my brother and a whole lot of boys my brother's age."

I could not have been more afraid for him, of watching him being taken away in a van and spending nights being tortured in a police station. He seemed so pleased and proud of himself that for a minute he took no notice of my concern. Then, as if he had been hearing my mind racing, he added confidently:

"They'll never catch us. You know what we did? We went at night and just flew out of there before anyone had a chance to call the police. No one knows who did it."

Everyone, of course, had heard about the burning of the post office. It was a government building and there were few of them standing at this point, so instead of being shocked by the news you would be surprised that it had not been demolished earlier. It was just a sign of the times—everything owned by the government was up for complete destruction. The comrades were damaging everything around them as a cry out for help, a way of sending a message to the government telling them to get us out of there. It had become clear that the high-school students—the ones who were at that point feeling that the streets were not enough for them, the ones who had begun to understand how trapped we all were in the *lekeishenes*—were the ones screaming and seething. But I was still thinking that we—me and Tshepo and Thato and everyone else our age—were still caught up in our own innocence, so that conversation was pointing out that I was wrong and this was deeply saddening and painful. The riots were now taking someone away from me, they were coming right into my own backyard.

Tshepo said bitterly, "Do you know how many people are being killed in prisons everyday for breaking stupid laws?"

He was pointing to his work, his defiant drawings. Just then Thato joined us. She sat down eating a grape-flavoured ice-pop and said, "When we went to Durban, I went walking down the beach and everyone was staring and staring at me, but I didn't know what was wrong until this White man walked up to me and said, 'This is not for you, turn around and walk that way, that side is for you.' I had been excited to have found a clean beach until he said that and I saw that he meant for me to go on the other side of the boardwalk, the side littered with paper cups and broken glass. Did you know you can't walk on the same side of the beach as White people?"

I did not know that because I had never been to a beach. But I had no idea why Thato had brought up that story. Maybe she just wanted to show Tshepo that he was not the only one who knew what was going on outside of the township, maybe she was saying she also knew a thing or two about the law. Whatever the reason was, I thought she brought up her story at a most inopportune time because all it did was fuel Tshepo's mind when all I wanted was for him to calm down and change the subject.

"And who cleans their side?" Tshepo asked, sounding bitter and not at all surprised.

"Maybe they don't throw glass and dirt on their beach," I said

"You didn't see them eating?" Tshepo asked Thato, whose lips and tongue were turning purple from the grape ice.

"They ate," she responded.

"So where did they throw their bottles and plastic containers?"

"Maybe in the rubbish bins."

"Were there rubbish bins on the Black side of the beach?"

"No, just like there are no rubbish bins *here*, only in town," Thato answered.

"*Malome* Joseph cleans streets in town, that's his job." Tshepo's voice was sounding agitated. "Do you think they don't have cleaners on the beaches?"

This was the first time Tshepo had not spoken about his Uncle Joseph with pride. Before, when he spoke of how his uncle was working in *town*, it was with that same admiration that some people had for men and women who worked for White people.

I felt a rush of distress. There was a lump in my throat even though I knew I was not about to cry, because I hardly ever did. I felt very uneasy hearing this from a close friend instead of an older comrade with whom I had no personal relationship. I could fantasise about being involved in the riots, but I was not ready for it to be so real. I still wanted it to be a world I knew very little about so that I could not think of someone I loved being that person the police came looking for in the middle of the night. Worst of all, Tshepo could have sounded like he was repeating someone else's speech, which would have been typical of him. But what scared me was how he sounded like he had given all this a lot of thought. He was not just an observer, but an ANC comrade himself. It was unnerving that someone so young would be in the middle of all that. It was hard for me to make sense of the sudden change in him.

At home I found Keitumetse sitting on the back *stoep* eating bread with peanut butter and drinking tea.

"*Tee?*" I said, meaning "isn't it too hot for that?"

"*Jaanong?*" My sister, in her teenage years, said little more than "*Jaanong* (so?)?" and "Leave me alone". Usually I would ignore her and go speak with someone more interesting, but today I needed her too much. I needed answers.

"You know what Tshepo showed me?" No response to my question, but I persisted. "He showed me how to make a petrol bomb!"

"How does he know?" she asked without a hint of interest.

"Mohau taught him"

A year before that Keitumetse had gotten interested in spending time alone with Mohau. The mention of his name always caught her interest and seemed to make her very excited. I could have sworn she was suppressing a smile.

"Mohau?" she said softly.

"*Ja,* Tshepo said they were the ones who bombed the post office."

My sister seemed impressed instead of appalled. She chewed the last bit of her peanut butter sandwich and turned to face me.

"Really? *Iyooo!* Bo-Mohau."

"He's dangerous!" I was getting frustrated; this was not what I had been hoping for. I wanted her to share my sadness, to see that we were losing friends here and that meant we all had to be afraid.

"I knew about the rent office, I didn't know about the post-office."

"The rent office!" I felt betrayed, how could I not have known any of this?

"Relax, Tihelo. You'd think they'd burnt your own house, eh!"

"But Tshepo is so young. He's a boy, not a comrade!" I protested.

"*Ja* . . . but it's the young boys who are burning places these days, I'm not surprised. But he should be careful, they're beating them all the time, the dogs don't care how old you are."

Her response only made me feel worse. I didn't want to know they were being beaten on the streets. It was all just going from bad to worse. There were more gunshots at night, more police vans during the day, and I seemed to be the only one who was still afraid. Both Tshepo and Keitumetse were very calm about all this. So I walked out the yard and did what comforted me the most at that time. I sat on the ground at the gate playing with rocks, grouping them into little families and telling stories to myself:

Mother rock: *This is my house! You can use that kind of language when you have your own house, but not while you're living under my own roof!*

Teenage rock: *Mama, I am a woman now, I can do whatever I want, and if you don't let me speak the way I want I will leave!*

Mother rock: *Then leave! Get out of my house and you can come back when you've learnt some manners.*

"Don't you ever get out of the sun?" I heard a voice that startled me as I was getting more absorbed in my story. My hand froze and clenched on to the mother rock. I was too afraid to look up because I had never heard that voice before. It was scratchy and deep but I knew it was a woman because the leather sandals in front of my hand were women's shoes.

Slowly, I looked up at the legs with the dry skin, the green dress just above the knees, and the slightly protruding stomach. My eyes stopped there for a second, Mother rock slipped from my wet palms and hit the ground. My knees gave way and my body dropped suddenly as I fell back on my buttocks. What was she doing here, standing so close? Mama would be furious if she were to come at this moment. I should run away—no, I should tell *her* to go away . . . but she had spoken! Who had heard her speak before? I started to move further away, walking backwards on my palms.

"Mamaka will be here very soon!"

"Mama *hao*? Your mother? Ha!" she said with a sarcastic laugh.

"Yes, she said not to speak to you," I warned her. But she replied: "Of course she did!"

"Tihelo!" Keitumetse called from behind me. "Come inside, get in the house now!"

Mma Kleintjie whispered, "I'm not afraid of your mother," and stood there staring at my sister, who of course stared right back. I got up and ran into the house. I think they both stood there and just stared at each other with neither one of them saying a word, until Keitumetse must have realised she was not supposed to be staring at an adult and walked back into the house.

At night I was uncomfortable. The heat made it impossible to sleep and I was vacillating between being frightened at how Mma Kleintjie had surprised me and appeared out of nowhere, and being disappointed that I had not gotten a good look at her face. Part of me wanted to go back and talk to her some more, look at her face. I kept asking myself what she had meant by "of course she did" because after all, she hardly knew my mother. I also felt guilty about looking so afraid of her, because I imagined that she got that a lot with everyone around her and it probably didn't help her get out of the house. Then again if she sneaked up on people like that all the time I was not surprised that she was considered to be a dubious figure around here.

It had been a full day. First the conversation with Tshepo and then

Mma Kleintjie. It left me with too many questions. Most of all, I felt younger and younger. I was really afraid for Mohau and Tshepo, wanting them to watch all the rioting and boycotting from a distance, the way I preferred to.

✳

I always thought that when I got older, when I would finish school and leave the township, I would be a journalist. I wanted to travel around the world and take pictures of people and the places they live in. I would write their stories and appear on television, reporting what I saw and heard. I always told Mama my dream on those nights when she came home long after the sun had set, having just got off the train. After she had been standing in the third class carriage all the way from Marabastad train station to Mabopane train station. A journey of about an hour. She would tell me about standing with her nose in some man's armpit all that way in a carriage so packed that people were hanging out the open doors of the train. Some nights the three of us would sit outside on the stoep while she stretched her legs and my sister rubbed them in soothing oil. We would laugh about whose armpit she had had the privilege of smelling that evening or how she had forgotten her train ticket and had to sneak into the station through a large hole in the fence to get onto the train.

Those nights were calm and tender. If they were summer nights we would be sitting on our front stoep to escape the indoor heat. Keitumetse and I would tell our mother who we would become. Keitumetse would be a nurse, just like Mama had wanted to be, and I would speak of being a journalist.

"What are you going to write about?" Mama would ask.

"I'm going to be on television!"

"Then what are you going to report?"

"Stories. Like what achieving independence feels like in Kenya. Or what women do for money in other lands. How Black Americans live, maybe. I want to see Brazil. I want to go everywhere!"

"Then go! Come back and tell me what they eat in Brazil or what Black people are like in America. Come back and tell me everything. We'll have a TV and I'll call all the neighbours to come and see my child. I'll say, 'That's my child right there, she's seeing the world'."

She would come with me to the Brazil of my imagination, or the hospitals and clinics of my sister's fantasies. We would go there together, night after night, laughing and hoping. They were so warm and welcoming, those places, you would never want to leave.

4

ON THE BLACK-AND-WHITE television at Thato's house there were no signs of the turmoil we were living in. Mr T and the A-team were building a fabulous reputation as the men who saved the day. We would enter their world for the exhilaration and inspiration that lasted an entire evening. The next day we would return for an hour of *Dimilione Tsa Kiriri* (The Millions of Kiriri), a TV3 drama in Sepedi about a group of men who leave their homes and travel for hundreds of kilometres to a place called Kiriri, where they search for a trunk full of millions—money that had supposedly been left there for decades. Television was a world we escaped into, it was the enviable, luxurious world of other people. A world we had grown up to think was someday coming our way. Whether consciously or subconsciously, all of us expected to walk into that world before getting too old. For hours after we watched a show we would talk incessantly about it, recounting what we had seen to each other as if we were speaking to someone who had not seen any of it.

The day after my conversation with Tshepo, the days after an evening of *The A-Team*, Thato and I were discussing the change we both saw in him. She was just as mystified as I was, both of us wondering when he had started becoming so involved in the freedom fighting. I was relieved that Thato seemed just as concerned as I was, and we agreed that we would speak with him about it. Her and I thought of ourselves as the know-it-all girls of the township sometimes. We would sit and discuss something we thought needed our attention and then agree to go and make it right. Our meetings were crucial, it was as if the state of the world depended on our actions and opinions.

We took ourselves very seriously. After discussing the Tshepo issue, it was time for me to bring up my more intriguing news.

"Mma Kleintjie spoke to me yesterday!" I started.

"Ah!" Thato covered her mouth with her hand, "*A reng?* What did she say?"

"She was so terrifying, like Mma Senyoro," I said, referring to a television character from another Sepedi drama, an evil woman who had gone around her township babysitting for people and then stealing babies after their parents had gone to work. Mama had told me it was really an insulting portrayal of black women in the townships, but I thought that she would not mind me using it about someone she disapproved of so much anyway.

"You know, I never said so before because it would have frightened us too much at the time, but I think there are similarities between Mma Senyoro and Mma Kleintjie. They both hate children but they are always watching them, and they both live alone and don't talk to people around them."

"Hmmm. But Mma Kleintjie never ever speaks to anyone and Mma Senyoro goes around looking for babysitting jobs," I was thinking out loud.

"Well, she spoke to you—*iyoooo!* Did you . . . I think you should tell *mama hao* so that she can tell Mma Kleintjie to stay away from you."

"I don't think she spoke to me because she needed anything."

"Maybe she needs to trap you and hide you under her bed like all her *ditloutlwane*," Thato said. It was all too chilling for me. What if Mma Kleintjie really did want to lock me up like one of her slaves? This was beginning to add a whole new dimension to my fear.

"You should tell Mama *hao*. You still haven't told me, what did she say?"

"She said: 'don't you ever get out of the sun?' and I fell on my back."

"*Iyooo*", Thato was sounding more afraid than I was. "She's been watching you."

"*Ha-e* (no). She watches all of us! I know she watches me . . . us, but I didn't think she would come so close. I'm becoming curious about her again like I was before."

"Leave her alone, she could take you and we would never see you again."

At this we jumped onto each other and hugged tightly. We did that often when we were both afraid, as if to protect each other.

"OK", Thato said as she let go of me, "let's talk about something else so we won't be so scared."

"OK," I said, feeling calmer from the hug. So I suggested we talk about the upcoming year and the transition into high school. We had been looking forward to going into the same school and I wanted to talk about going to register—the first time we would be doing it without our parents. We were lying on her garden chairs on her front lawn sipping cold Oros Orange Juice. Her mother had mixed it up for us and given us some biscuits to go with it and I was feeling pampered and pleased as ever. At least, I thought, this is bound to get us excited because it was something we had been looking forward to and fantasizing about since our second last year in primary school.

"Mama says Matseke is the best school because the principal really keeps students in order. That's where Keitumetse is and she says it's really strict," I said, head in the sun and feeling the cool of the juice down my throat. Thato was sitting completely in the shade of the apricot tree that stood in the middle of the lawn.

"My parents think I should go to Matseke too, but my father just heard something about the White Catholic schools being opened to Black people and maybe I'll go there if it's true. Isn't that exciting?!"

I was devastated. Not only had I never imagined going to a different school than Thato, I knew there was no way that Mama could afford to send me to a school in town. It was just impossible. How could this be happening? I asked myself. The glass of juice was becoming too heavy for my shaking hand, but I tried to sound like she had just said: "It's sunny, isn't it?" to which I lazily replied—after placing the glass on the ground—"Yes it is!"

The reality of it was that if anyone could have gone to those schools, it was Thato. She was one of those people whose families were doing so well financially that the only reason she was in a Black school was because she had to be. If the White schools were opening up for us then that was where she would go— there was no 'maybe' about it.

I told myself to calm down, the beginning of the year was still weeks away. We were not even at Christmas yet, my summer days would be long and I would savour every minute of it. However, to my horror, Thato seemed more excited about the prospect of going to a White school than she was sad. There was no mention of how she would miss me, not a single word about our unwritten and unspoken expectations of each other. I felt like I was the only one who felt upset. Where was all this change going anyway? First Tshepo was beginning to sound like I had never known him and now Thato was leaving me here, alone and afraid. I wanted to probe some more, to ask her if she felt the slightest bit of sadness at the thought of going into class everyday and not seeing my face. I kept thinking, won't it break your heart to have me waiting at your gate every morning, wearing the same uniform, carrying the same kind of school bag and ready for us to walk together?

I did not ask because I felt like she was too excited to care, as she should have been. Any of us would choose being driven into town every morning over walking with polished shoes on a dusty road. Who was not curious about what it meant to be around White people everyday? To speak their language and laugh with them and go into their houses? As for myself, I had only ever been in a White home once and that had been when I was about four years old and Mama had taken me to the house of the family she worked for at the time. I remember how grand it was, with many rooms and a large swimming pool outside. I remember wanting to run around and go into every room because I was so excited, but Mama had kept me sitting and playing quietly outside, playing alone until it was time to go home. I did not enjoy it as much as I would have liked to because in retrospect, Mama seemed too determined to keep me quiet and polite and that must have meant that my presence there was making everyone uncomfortable. However, I imagined that it would be a whole different feeling if you were going in with one of the children.

It must feel more welcoming if you were wearing the same school uniform, if you read the same books and understood the language on the television as much as they did. It must be fun if you could laugh and laugh at one of those shows where there is an audience laughing in the background. I could hardly contain my distress just thinking about it all happening without me. My best friend would start a new life and share it with someone other than myself. My mind was stuck on the future, dreading it. I had not realised how quiet I had become until Thato shook my arm.

"Tihelo! I said, there's Tshepo."

"Where?" I sat up straight on the chair.

"There, going to buy ice. Let's call him."

"Tshepo!" We shouted in unison, and he turned around to make continuous circles with his forefinger, a township sign that meant he would be back in a minute.

Five minutes later he walked out of the house where they sold ice, sucking on an orange ice-block, and headed our way. He walked in and sat at the end of Thato's chair.

"Did you know it's Black Christmas this year?" He began enthusiastically, as he sucked on his ice.

"What is that?" I inquired.

"Black Christmas means we boycott town. No one buys anything from the White stores, only from stores around here. So no big Christmas presents. We're blocking the highways to town from the twenty third to the day after New Year's."

Oh God, I thought. No Christmas presents? Everyone's mood would probably be so sullen. And for what? This was really getting to be too much. I was apprehensive and fearing the worst. I could not imagine the comrades being quiet about their boycott either. My mind came back to Thato's voice.

"Tshepo, you have to stop being so involved in riots and boycotts. The police will beat you and lock you up," She looked to me for support.

"*Ja,*" I added weakly. "They beat boys your age a lot. Keitumetse told me."

"Tshepo, you could get hurt. Why don't you just stay away from your brother's friends? You don't come play with us lately."

Tshepo was obviously not taking any of this in. "As long as there are comrades in Exile, as long as Mandela, Thambo and Sisulu are still in jail, we the people . . ."

He was doing it again, sounding like he was repeating someone else's words at first and then sounding like they came from his heart. I wanted him to stop, to just sit there and talk about his drawings or forbidden adventures that him and Peter and all the other boys had had before. So I tried to bring back the side of him I knew better. I interrupted him and started talking about street football, rounders, and the times we had climbed over other people's fences to reach their lemon and apple trees.

I tried and tried to remind him of being a child again, which of course was my own attempt at escaping the horrors unfolding in our lives. It was obvious that Tshepo was feeling none of our fears. Instead, he spoke over and over again about the plans to burn tires in the middle of the road so that no one would be able to drive. We heard about the bombing of buildings in town, about how it was all part of a plan to have us living the lives that White people were living, and about how, if Thato and I knew our place in this world, we would participate in the plan. Eventually Thato and I gave up trying and told him we wanted time alone to talk about girl things. He then left saying he had a meeting to go to that evening, and we felt utterly exhausted with fear.

5

THE TEMPERATURES WERE rising higher and the days getting longer. The rains dug holes in the streets at night, and the sun was scorched the earth during the day. Our feet got scalded if we walked or attempted to play on the streets, so we sought refuge under large trees in our backyards. Most of us would gather together in the shade to tell stories with small stones or would just lie there together sharing gossip, discussing the latest township events or even talking about far-away lands we would visit after high school, those places we were planning our lives in. From the time we had known each other, we had understood without saying anything, that none of us were planning our lives in the township. Everyone spoke of other places when they talked about growing up. It was like an unspoken agreement that we were born believing in other, far away worlds.

People would take turns going to buy ice blocks, which would be melting all over the messenger by the time he or she got back to the meeting place. We would hold the dripping treats with desperation as they temporarily cooled our throats and then we would sit and wait for someone to come up with an idea to get more money for buying more ice. Sometimes someone would have gotten twenty cents from a visiting uncle or a grandmother who had just spent an entire day sitting and waiting outside some government office for her pension money. Karabo's mother had a tuck shop, a little convenience store in her garage where she sold bread, cool drinks, cans of baked beans, spaghetti and meatballs, as well as sweets and potato chips. While she worked in town, her sister—Karabo's aunt—ran the tuck shop. If Karabo helped her behind the till, she would get about fifty cents, which bought ten pieces of ice—enough for almost all of us to each have our own piece.

For my sister and I, the lazy hours under apricot trees were coming to an end. One Sunday night when Mama was in the kitchen ironing her work uniform—a pink and white striped dress and a matching apron—she announced that she had other plans for us.

"You do nothing but talk nonsense under those trees," she said irritably, wrinkling her forehead. "I spoke to your aunt in Johannesburg and she and I will see to it that you spend these holidays doing something useful."

Keitumetse, who was gaining furious boldness, demanded, "And what would you have us do then? I'm not doing anything with the relatives this year."

My mother almost dropped the iron on the coal stove. She put her fists on her hips and I began to move towards the door.

"Keitumetse, there's three women in this house and only one of us is a mother. Are you the mother?"

To my horror, I thought I saw my sister's eyes roll all the way up to her eyebrows. While Mama and I watched in horror, Keitumetse did not say a word and was obviously not feeling my fear.

"I said, are you the mother?" my mother repeated herself, moving closer to Keitumetse, who sat straightening her hair with a hot comb.

Oh, no! I thought. I had one foot outside the kitchen door and my body was headed towards the bedroom.

"Mama . . ." she protested.

"I will decide what you do and don't do this summer, and it won't be sitting talking about none-of-your-business under large trees or holding hands with Mohau."

That zipped my sister's lips right up. There was no way she was going to deny that she had something going on with Mohau and she certainly did not want to hear about it from Mama's lips.

"The two of you are spending too much time around those boys. Boys will make you dirty, they'll get you in the worst kind of trouble".

Even I knew what kind of trouble that was. I mean, I had no idea how exactly they got you into it but I knew that they had a major role in making girls have to go to their aunts' homes in the rural areas for a long time. Some girls around here had been known to miss a whole year of school because of that kind of trouble. They had to repeat classes when they got back from their aunts. Thato and I had talked about how we wanted nothing to do with that kind of trouble. Keitumetse, on the other hand, seemed not so afraid. Something about Mohau made her spend about an entire morning in front of the mirror before she would dare to step out of the house. Sometimes I had to tell her if Mohau was on the street before she would decide what to wear. She would sweep the dusty yard in some of her best clothes if he was out there. It was very strange and annoying. Worst of all, all of it seemed sudden. It felt as if Keitumetse had changed overnight. One day she could not care less about bruised knees and playing barefoot. Everyone told me I was soon to know what she was feeling, but the thought of Mama ever looking at me with that much disapproval made me cringe.

Obviously Mama was having long conversations with the neighbours, because for someone who spent everyday of the week working in town, she knew a lot about how we were spending our days.

"Tihelo you should also start staying away from those boys. I won't have my children learning to make petrol bombs. I have no time to go looking for people in prison."

"I didn't make a petrol bomb," I said with as much innocence as I could manage to work into my voice.

"Stay away from that park," Mama said, giving me a look that made the discussion final. I was about to let out a sigh when Keitumetse added, "Mma Kleintjie came here the other day. She was talking to Tihelo and I told her to leave but she just stood there and—"

This time my mother's fingers must have gone limp and given way because from the sound of the iron hitting the floor, I knew it was not deliberately thrown. It was a lazy and slow clank! The hot metal landed on its side and only a few inches away from Mama's foot.

"What . . . What was she doing here? Tihelo!! What did she say to you? What did you say to her? Did I not tell you never ever . . . ever to speak to that woman? Ever!"

"I told her you were coming. I told her you didn't want me talking to her." I was pleading, angry with Mma Kleintjie for coming close to me.

"What did she say? Tell me. Tell me everything."

"Mama she didn't say anything. She just told me to get out of the sun—that's all."

She paused and stared at me. I thought she was really angry but for some reason her face looked more hurt than angry. She told me to go and get ready for bed, her voice much calmer. I could not have been happier to leave that kitchen.

In bed I thought I could hear Mama telling Keitumetse to watch me.

"That woman should never speak to either one of you. She's not to be trusted. Just do me that favour, please"

Three days later a strange man appeared on our back door with two large bags filled with popsicles.

"This is for you," he said, handing my sister and I the yellow Checkers bags. I gave him a glass of water. He thanked me politely, said goodbye, and was quickly on his way.

So this was the plan. Mama had arranged for us to sell popsicles, which meant that we had to stay home all day in case someone came to buy. That night she set the rules: we were not to have more than two friends over at a time. Under no circumstances were we to leave the house. Bread and milk were to be bought at the beginning of each day so that we would not be running to the shops in the middle of the day. We had to close the gate and stop selling after dark. Meanwhile, I was asked to make a sign for the gate letting everyone know that we were now in business. It was a plan guaranteed to keep us away from the streets until we got back to school. Thato would come and play everyday, but sometimes she had to go and see what everyone else was up to since you could only do so much playing in the same yard day after day. I resented my mother and felt like she had locked us up, taken away our freedom. Still, I did nothing against her rules because I feared her wrath more than I valued sucking on an ice block in the shade.

6

BY THE TIME Christmas came around the streets were quiet and eerie. Everyone had heard about the comrades' call for a boycott of White stores, and all of us had stayed home to avoid peril. It was the least festive Christmas I had ever had: no parties, no new clothes, and it seemed like hardly anyone had gone away on holiday. Thato told me that three comrades had come to her house to warn her parents against going away and spending their money at White people's businesses. Mohau and Tshepo's mother was back for two weeks, her only break from the kitchens and the only time she spent with her family all year, because her *missies* wanted her there to clean and cook whenever they needed her assistance.

I appreciated the fact that Mama came home every day, even if we really only saw her briefly each day—if we saw her at all. That Christmas she cooked chicken and rice, which were just about the only two things that let you know there was something special about the day. We rarely had chicken, except for Sundays, and rice usually meant you had some money to spare because it was a lot more expensive than cornmeal. I was especially upset about the mood around me—it was like collective mourning. People sat outside and listened to slow Sunday blues on the radio at relatively low volume. It was my first Black Christmas, a very significant time in my growing up. I thought of friends I was losing, since both Thato and Tshepo would be taking different routes from myself. Our years of childhood innocence were coming to an abrupt end that year.

Mama could sense that I was feeling unhappy, and she tried to cheer me up by promising to make us custard and pudding, another rare and special treat in our house. I sat with her and Keitumetse at our kitchen table, listening to music and the sound of our spoons hitting the plates. None of us said more than two words to each other. Later in the afternoon it began to feel like one of those days that are sure to either turn sour or exhilarating, and at that point I was feeling so sad and upset that I was ready for it to go either way. Sure enough, a riot broke out and there was a long march on the main road, but the comrades never made their way to our streets. All we heard was the singing, but because we had to stay at home and wait for customers we never got to see the faces from which the voices were emanating.

So many arrests were made that by the time New Year's Day came around, it felt like only half the parents on our street knew where their children were. Mohau was definitely in jail, someone had seen him taken away. Tshepo was home because he had apparently managed to escape, but he was covered in bruises and had minor cuts on his legs. His face betrayed so much fear and loathing, it was hard to look at him without feeling uneasy. One would have thought years had passed since our day in the sun at Thato's house. Seeing him like that only made me resent his newfound interest more. He was growing up and becoming a very bitter man, while I still wanted him to be the boy I had grown up with.

✳

The new school year could not have come around fast enough. Thato spent the first few months refusing to say a word in Setswana because she said she was forbidden to speak her language at Ascension Convent, her new school. Only English was allowed, and the nuns never ran out of punishments for those who did not obey this rule. I could not keep up with her in conversation since my English was very limited, so our friendship began to quickly slide downhill. She would even pronounce our names with an English accent, calling me "T-hay-low," and herself just "T." She was known as "T-girl" in her new circle of friends. These were friends I had no interest in, and I stayed away from her house more and more—partly because I could not communicate with them and partly because they sounded extremely annoying speaking from their nasal passages.

I also tired of hearing about the perks of being in the so-called "multiracial" schools. It made me feel small. I said nothing about how our school's windows were broken, how we cleaned our own classes, or how the constant boycotts kept us at home. Unlike the "multiracial" schools, we still had corporal punishment. I had got used to hearing the sound of gunshots in the middle of the day and was constantly terrified—that, and I could smell tear gas miles away. Thato suddenly called us "disruptive" and "unwilling" to go to school. I wished that I could go where she went every day, because it took her far enough away from my reality that she was able to have a very distorted idea of what went on around here. I hated what I lived, so that whenever I was angry with riots and tired of hiding in people's backyards, I agreed with her. At those times I thought the students were very disruptive and that they never wanted to spend any amount of time in the classroom. I was learning very little in school, apart from what exit was closest to my classroom and the fastest way to get home from school when it was raining tear gas. I did not feel very close to anyone and had not made any friends yet. High school was very lonely. Life was suddenly very adult-like, and adulthood was taxing.

One day Tshepo, who was now in the same school as I, suggested that we work together on making T-shirts and fliers to help the comrades publicize their meetings and rallies. I wanted something to do that would bring results, having had no homework for weeks, and so I made it clear to Tshepo that I would not participate in any of the events and that under no circumstances was my mother to know what was going on. I also desperately wanted to stay close to Tshepo after all this time. Thato and I were hardly good friends any more and I was still only half-interested in being very close to Karabo. So I set some conditions before I agreed to help, and we began a project that was to change my perspective of the riots. At six o'clock every morning, after Mama had left to catch the five-thirty train, Tshepo would be at my door waiting to take me to the comrades' offices. His grandfather thought we had Bible class in the morning, like we used to in primary school, and when my mother asked, I repeated the same story. She was slightly suspicious, and gave me a lecture about how she hoped never to find out that I had not told the truth, but after that she never said another word about it.

We walked for twenty minutes to a house on the outskirts of the township that looked like any other four-room. I had expected it to have some sort of sign outside, or at least a detectable aura around it that let you know you had reached the headquarters of the ANC student movement, the South African Students Organization, or SASO. There was a very well kept lawn in the front yard and no high wall or anything that looked like the owners needed to tighten security. In fact, you would have thought it was just another quiet family home. Tshepo told me on the way over that they would know we were coming as no one ever dropped by without calling first and if they did, they would have to say a code word, which even he did not know. Also, whoever was in the house would spot us long before we approached the house. Someone was always standing guard.

Every morning Tshepo and I would walk in wearing black and white, every township school's uniform. At the door we would meet a tall boy who looked to be about my sister's age. He always wore a yellow T-shirt that said "Release Mandela" on the front, with the face of the prisoner above the words. Every morning he would say, "Viva ANC viva!" and we would respond, "Viva!"

I felt very uneasy in that house. Sometimes I was even terrified. Everyone was so warm and welcoming, and they all treated us like their younger siblings, affectionately calling Tshepo and I "fellow comrades." It was not that I did not like them, because I did. I looked up to the women, who seemed to command a lot of respect from the men, and who were equally busy planning events and meetings. I also liked the kitchen aromas of baked bread and coffee, which the comrades always offered us. It was just that unlike the outside, the inside of the house felt uncomfortable because I was always aware that we were in the middle of something precarious. It was as if we were jumping up and down at the edge of a cliff. Everyone spoke in very low tones. People would ask us to keep our voices reasonably low once we were in the house. I always feared that at any minute the police would burst in and raid the house. It was as if we were treading on a minefield.

I reluctantly consented to the comrades' request that for six months before the winter holidays in June I would go there every morning with Tshepo to make fliers. He would decorate them, using his drawing skills, and I would write what events were taking place as well as what had taken place at the previous event. Sometimes I would help Thabang—the boy with the "Release Mandela" T-shirt —with the newsletter. We would have to mention any lost or jailed comrades on every flier, and the number of people who disappeared or who were imprisoned increased tremendously in the time that I was there. By February Mohau had been released from prison, but instead of going home he went into hiding. Tshepo missed him sorely but was never allowed to know where his brother was, although a woman called Dikeledi occasionally brought news of how Mohau was doing, as well as little messages for Tshepo and Keitumetse. Writing notes would have been too risky.

Over the first two months I admitted to myself that my fear of going to the headquarters was becoming a little too overwhelming. I had to decide if I was going to continue going there every morning, or if I was only going to go every few days. The problem was that there really was a lot of work to be done, and I had made a commitment by agreeing to be there until the winter. I decided to tell Keitumetse where I had been going. She would not tell Mama as long as I let her go out and not help sell ice-pops on weekends. She did not seem as concerned as I had expected, which made me think I may have been a little bit paranoid, but it also made me feel somewhat safer to think that someone at home knew where I was every morning for two hours before school. I also realized that one good thing about working at the headquarters was that I was always up to date on what march or rally was coming up, and it made me feel less on edge and apprehensive.

Around that time I began making friends with Lebo, the girl I shared a desk with in class. We had very little in common, but I thought she was very funny and smart. She was a dancer and cared about little else. The best thing about her was that she made me laugh really hard all the time. Mama only sort of liked her and said it made her uneasy that I was getting close to a girl who invited boys into her home when her father was not there. It was something that also bothered me about Lebo, but I was not about to share that with my mother. I thought of her as *sekhebereshe*, a derogatory word used for women who love the company of men openly and shamelessly. I suppose intimacy and affection with men intimidated me; I thought of men as people who could very easily be the end of my dreams. That was something I had got from my mother.

She would say, "No one in this house will have an abortion."

I would imagine myself pregnant, sitting and dreaming about the person I could have been. This lack of choice came up in many different areas of my life, sometimes leaving me angry, but most of the time I was just fearful. Even the simple choice of whether or not I wanted to kiss a boy was something that took a lot of thinking. It brought to mind pregnant women my age who had let go of the possibility of leaving the township. None of us had different options. You could not decide whether you would have or not have a baby. The law allowed no reproductive choices for women, Black or White.

We also did not have much information about our bodies, sex, or pregnancy. None of this information was available to us through our parents, and there was no such thing as a library in the township, or even within a hundred kilometres of where we lived. Sex was the killer of dreams. I had never heard about a man and a woman loving each other. All you heard about men and women was how, when they encountered each other, they found a way to sabotage each other's futures. In some girls, like myself, this kind of talk brought out fear, and in others it brought out curiosity. I was frightened of my sexuality, but Lebo relished hers. Her attitude made me uneasy about her, so I did what is always easiest to do and chose an offensive word to call her in my mind. This was in an effort to feel better about myself.

Lebo knew nothing about me going to the SASO offices every day. I kept it secret because I was obliged to do so, but also because I did not have the same amount of trust in her as I had had in Thato. She was a very new friend, and for that reason I held back a lot. I kept all kinds of things to myself in those days. It was lonely and hard, because I felt so many things that seemed to weigh me down. It may have made it just a little bit easier to have had someone to talk to, but I could not decide who that could be. I was still pining over Thato, secretly wishing she would come knocking at my door and ask how my life was going. I would sit for hours by myself, watching the leaves turn in autumn and the sun set earlier, all the while wishing I was spending time with the only best friend I had ever had. Sometimes I would speak with Keitumetse about my friendship with Thato, but she would just be irritable and tell me Thato did not deserve me. Perhaps she felt a need to protect me, but it did not help. My heart was heavy and I always fell asleep as soon as I got home from school, which meant that I never got any time with Mama. She missed me so much she started waking me at half past four in the morning before she left for work, just so she could have a minute with me. She had always hated waking us up, but she said it was beginning to feel like she never knew how I was, and that bothered her.

One morning I sat up and spoke to her for a few minutes longer than usual. I told her that high school was difficult and that I was finding it hard to constantly have to leave school in the middle of the day because of the riots and demonstrations. Because these activities involved mostly high-school students, I had never felt it to the same extent when I was in middle school.

"I have a better idea now why people are rioting, but I find it hard to keep up in school. The teachers don't even demand anything from us anymore," I groaned.

"I would take you out of there if I could. You know that. We just don't have that choice, just like with everything else." She gave me a very apologetic look.

"I know, Ma. I just wish it wasn't so hard. I feel like we're hardly ever in class anymore."

"You know, it might make you feel better to think that if you didn't choose to rebel against Bantu education you would probably be resigning yourself to a life of despair. At least this way you're saying you want it to be better than this. Maybe look at it that way, okay?"

"Okay," I said, lying back on the pillow. I will think of it that way and see if that helps a little, I thought.

It helped a little bit and made me feel less alone for about two, maybe three hours. But I was still worried about the prospect of eventually leaving school without good enough marks to make it into journalism at a good university.

That day I decided to try and let my friendship with Lebo grow a little bit more, partly because I was desperate and there was really no one else to talk to. So I went to visit her at her home. I went to SASO in the morning and then walked up to her house later, which was closer to the office than it was to my house. She was surprised to see me, maybe even less than thrilled. It was never a problem to just drop by someone's house and say hello, so I didn't really understand what her problem was. Instead of inviting me inside she started to walk me out to the gate, saying she was busy cooking for her father.

"You know, I've never met your father," I said, hinting that maybe this was the time to do that.

"I know, but he's sleeping now so you'll see him another time," she said.

"Okay." I was just about to make a quick exit when a man came growling around the corner. He had a beer can in one arm and his other arm ended in a round, ball-like shape below his elbow.

"So where's my food?" he demanded angrily.

"*Dumelang,*" I greeted him respectfully, but he paid no attention to me.

"I'll see you Monday in school," Lebo said and quickly ran to towards her father, who stood there staring at her bitterly. He still did not seem to have seen me.

I left their home and started walking back to mine, unsure of what to make of that encounter. It was the first time I had ever seen Lebo look so unhappy and disturbed. I felt sorry for her, but more than that I felt curious and wanted to know what was going on in her life outside of school. I must have assumed that she had a lot of money because she visited the hair salon at least once a week. She had also won dance competitions around the township and gone on to compete in big events with different schools, so I thought she was doing very well. Sometimes it is hard to know what people are living because they mask it so well, telling hilarious stories of what they do when you are not around. You might even go as far as envying them, if you were mesmerized by their voices and their laughter, their fabulous ability to tell a good story. You could never tell that they were living in utter despair.

Lebo's house looked and felt gloomy. There were no decorations, no garden, not even a *stoep*. It looked desperate, almost like no one lived there. Always thinking there was a story behind everything, I thought I'd go to Ausi Martha's house. She was always ready to divulge information about other people's lives—you could never spend more than ten minutes with her without finding out who was sick, dying, imprisoned, broke, or cheating. Of course, I had also spent years with her and knew nothing about what was going on in her own home, information she obviously deliberately withheld. She carried so much shame. I could never feel comfortable around shame, and I spent less and less time at her house because hers seemed to be growing with age.

I went over for a few minutes that day, however, because it was very impolite to not stop by the homes of neighbours every once in a while and ask how they are keeping, and see if they are sleeping and eating well. So from Lebo's house I started walking towards our street to give my greetings to Ausi Martha, hoping to see what I could learn about Lebo and her father.

✽

The woman walking up and down the streets selling the brooms she carries on her head comes with stories from afar. She carries those stories harder and heavier than the ten solid wooden brooms she bears so delicately on her head. She comes into my yard when I am sitting on the ground playing with my stones, the sun pressing onto the centre of my head, my neck burning. I am ten years old and I crave stories of people who have been here much longer than I have. I want to know about the men in the mines, and the women's histories. She comes in for a glass of water, puts her cane brooms down on the ground next to her body, and then sits at my side, her legs stretched out. I listen, she tells.

Yesterday she came with one about the woman who lost her home to the Group Areas Act, the law that says people have to live separate from those of a different skin colour.

"For years she had this dream of living in a big home, the kind with room for all her six children and an extra one she would use as a story room. She was the town's storyteller, people came from near and far and sat down at her feet to hear stories of Africans from all over. Tales of how groups of our ancestors moved down south from the northeastern lands. Of how many others were taken away across the ocean on White men's ships. Her stories made people laugh, sometimes they made them cry, but most of all, they told people about their own history, they were a way of getting to know their ancestors.

"She charged about five cents a story and saved the money in a secret place. Years later she finally built the house of her dreams, complete with the story room. People kept coming, sitting on the carpeted floor, resting their heads on the pillows, listening. Then one day, in the middle of the night as she slept, a storm of men in green uniforms with guns and large boots came in with a force she had no way of resisting. They told her, 'We got together and decided, you're not fit to be here. You and your

stories belong elsewhere. Take what you can and go, this is now our land.' And so it came to pass. They built a new town where her people had lived. Where they had come from all over to hear her tell the history of their foremothers. On that very land, they erected their own homes, as if the place was all new, as if they had discovered a new land where no one had lived before. They made it their home because they could, because it was the law. They had convinced themselves that it belonged to them and that they had come to take it from trespassers, so they saw the removals as a victory. They called the place Triumph.

"The women and her people were thrown onto foreign ground. Barren lands where no crops could grow. They lost their homes and everything that went with them. And if she or any of her people ever wished to walk that ground again, they had to carry papers that allowed her to do so."

"What happened to her children?" I ask, playfully rubbing two stones together. "Did she leave with them?"

"What does a hen do when you come near her chicks?" she responds, taking her last sip of water. She gets up, balances the brooms steadily on her head, and goes on her way.

7

I WAS RIGHT, Ausi Martha knew a lot about Lebo's house. Her father had worked in a steel factory for years and lost his arm to a fast-moving saw. He was about twenty-seven when this happened and it automatically meant losing his job. He came home days later to his wife and child, both of whom had been subsisting on his paycheque in addition to the mother's salary, which she earned cleaning rich people's houses up on the hill in the township. He came home burdened with bitterness. He carried so much hate it drove his wife right out of the township marked with bruises on her face and limbs. Tiptoeing around him had brought her nothing except closer to her death.

"The only thing he let that child keep was her dancing. He took away everything else," Ausi Martha told me, with a slight hint of laughter in her voice. This is how she was, it was such a pleasure and so easy for her to tell of other people's misfortunes that it almost made her laugh. Perhaps it made her think less about what was going on in her own home.

While on that subject, I decided to take a chance and bring up an old topic that I had been thinking about on and off for months.

"You know, Mma Kleintjie spoke to me a few months ago," I started.

"I heard," she said in a cool, disinterested voice.

"Do you know what she said to me?"

"I don't think you should be listening to anything that woman has to say."

"I was really startled, you know," I continued, despite her obvious lack of interest. "She just appeared right in front of me, I mean I didn't even hear her coming. One minute I was playing and the next minute she was right there."

"Well, you know, you're a big girl now, you should stop playing with rocks on the ground."

"I was thirteen," I said defensively. "Still, I like telling my stories, it's soothing. Anyway, I haven't told you what she said yet—"

"Your mother told me what she said. And as much as I hate that woman, she was right, you should stay out of the sun. You're lucky you're so light-skinned. Some of us have to spend a lot of money on creams just to look like you."

"I don't want to be so light, I don't look like anyone!"

"Tihelo!" she exclaimed, her emphatic tone telling me I should be ashamed of such thoughts.

"Why is she so interested in me anyway? She's always watching me."

"She's not just interested in you, she's like that with all the children."

"She has never come that close to any other child. She hates children." I was still calling myself a child even in high school, mainly because you cannot call yourself anything else. There is no term for older or younger children. We were all the same in the eyes of adults.

"You should stay away from her anyway."

"What do you know? Why is she so interested in me? Do you know why?"

"She's probably interested in you because you're as light-skinned as her and she doesn't like Black people, that's why. She probably finds it easier to look at you than it is to look at everyone else."

"Hmmm. That makes sense. I probably remind her of someone she knows or something. Like family, maybe."

"Maybe. She is a witch, you know about her," and she was whispering as she said this. "Don't go anywhere near her," she warned me.

That was enough information to suppress my interest in *Lekhalate* for a very long time. We went on to do a round of neighbourhood gossip. Mma Motsei up the street had got tired of her husband beating her, so she had splashed him with a pot full of hot water and he was now in the hospital. Her children were sick of him too, they were on her side. But still all of them went to visit him in the hospital like a good loving family. His wife brought him the food she cooked at home, and she and the children all sat by his side for three visiting hours every day reading him the newspaper and telling him what was going on in the outside world. No hard feelings, no distress. They wished him well and he was grateful for their time and love.

Three doors down, Thebe, who was probably the quietest and most mysterious man on our street, was making a lot of money from building large steel fences and gates and selling them to the rich people up on the hill. Soon, Ausi Martha was saying, he would be living right up there with them. We were all really fascinated by his talent, something he had never gone to school for. He had always been put things together his whole life. When he was in his mid-teens he had gone to town and worked for a White man who did the same thing, and he said that's how he perfected his skill. He watched how the White man was doing it for a while, quit his job after a few months, and went on to start his own business at home. Thato's parents had had him build their fence and large black steel gate. Thebe still lived with his parents and had built a room and a bathroom behind the parents' four-room. Ausi Martha thought it would be good to get him in her house, maybe make him some special tea and get him to notice one of her daughters. So far she had had no luck.

Across the street, Ausi Martha thought *Koko*, or Grandma, Diile was getting a little old for selling vegetables in town every day of the week. She thought she should cut down a little bit, maybe go only on weekdays and stay home on weekends.

"You know, since her husband died she feels like there's no reason to be home so much," Ausi Martha told me. "They gave her a lot of money at Checkers, but she still feels strongly about working. Women whose husbands worked at grocery stores get a lot of money."

Koko Diile's husband had died of diabetes when I was in my second last year of middle school. She had worn her black mourning clothes for a total of six months—Ausi Martha had counted—instead of doing the customary year of mourning. She raised a few eyebrows and had a lot of tongues wagging, but she filled her bags with vegetables she bought from the market and got in a taxi every morning to go to town. She went to Blood Street, where she sat on the sidewalk at the same spot and sold potatoes and tomatoes to men and women who worked in town. She never explained herself or apologized to anyone.

We sat and gossiped, asked questions about everyone else's lives except each other's, until it was time for me to go home. I never mentioned it to Ausi Martha, but I had heard from Keitumetse that her husband was not actually in Johannesburg as she would have had us believe, but living in a one-room shack in Block A, just across the main road. He had a new wife and the two of them were renting a space in a yard full of "tin houses," shacks made from corrugated iron. Once a year he visited and Ausi Martha talked about how he had come back from the factories, but in fact he had just taken a twenty-minute walk across the main road to bring his children their Christmas presents. He would spend the day sitting on a one-person bench in the shade, where he would accept nothing to drink or eat from his estranged wife. Everyone knew about Ausi Martha's special teas, because she bragged about her magic, and he wanted nothing to do with that. He would bring his own three bottles of beer and sit there drinking and pretended to have a good time, while Ausi Martha sat across from him wearing her best clothes. She would work her way down to the bottom of two litres of Sprite, completely unaware that she was not the one who ought to be carrying the shame. After all, the man had left his children without a cent while she had stayed and endured all the trials of single parenthood.

I arrived home to a dark, unlit house that Saturday evening at six o'clock, not suspecting the doom that was about to befall us. I found Keitumetse sitting outside, reading a letter from Mohau, the first one she had ever received since he had gone into hiding in February. She looked as if someone had been tickling her all day, not even aware that my arrival at that hour meant that it would take a while before she would have supper. I closed the curtains and turned on the lights. I found vegetables to cook and my sister came in the kitchen to keep me company.

"He says he thinks about me all the time. All the time. He can't wait to get back," Keitumetse told me as I stood there peeling potatoes and slicing onions.

"So when is he coming back? Does he know?" I asked. "No, actually, he doesn't. The police are looking for him and a group of other comrades he was arrested with. He will remain in hiding until he thinks they've decided he's not a threat anymore."

"What do they think he'll do?"

"Start a riot, I think. What else can they be afraid of?"

"You know, I never asked," I said, stopping for a moment. "What did they see him do on Christmas exactly? There were so many people but they arrested only a small group, much smaller than usual."

Keitumetse explained, "He was suspected of organizing the whole rally. The police see him as a leader now. I don't think they understand that there is no one leader at any given point, that people organize together and everyone has a different role."

"But the older students definitely have more prominent roles than the younger ones," I said, dropping my voice to a little whisper so that only she could hear me. "I mean, even at the office they tell us what to do. No one our age would ever be a leader."

"I know. He probably wasn't just sitting and taking orders from anyone. That just isn't his style," she said approvingly.

My sister really admired her boyfriend, she kept telling me that he was a man, not a boy. Frankly, I thought he was arrogant and bossy, but that was just me. The entire time I was cooking she was rereading his letter with a large grin and I had to concentrate hard on what I was doing because I found her excitement over Mohau was very annoying.

The train that left Pretoria station—the Black-only station—at half past six in the evening got to Mabopane station at half past seven. Mama would take a taxi from the station after stepping off the train and would be home by eight o'clock at the latest. But that unusually chilly April evening, my mother never came home.

Since starting high school my worry level had increased twofold. Whereas in middle school I could lie down and put my mind on something else when I felt uneasy, in high school I would panic and fidget, constantly looking outside for something reassuring. We ate standing and pacing around the house, wondering what was going on. Keitumetse suggested that we call Mama's *missies* but I felt uncomfortable doing that. I did not want to get on the phone and start speaking English. The people she worked for at the time were English-speaking and Mama said they really did not appreciate it when people spoke to them in Afrikaans, the only White language I felt I could speak somewhat well. My sister was really confident in her English as she was in just about everything she had learned in school, so she picked up the phone and I stood next to her with my ear touching the receiver so that I could listen to the conversation.

"Hello, can I please speak with Kgomotso?" she started after someone picked up the phone.

"Who?"

"Kgomotso. Please," Keitumetse said, raising her voice a little because she thought she was not clear.

"This is an English household. There is no one by that name here. Goodbye—"

"Sorry!" I interrupted quickly, remembering something and taking the receiver. "Gladys!" I said.

"What? Oh! Gladys. No, sorry, Gladys has gone home already. Why are you calling at this hour? Gladys doesn't work at night, she leaves very early." The woman on the other end of the line sounded very irritated. Just then a man's voice piped up in the background: "Why are Gladys's friends calling here? She's not supposed to use the phone when she's here, is she?"

The woman yelled back: "Steven, it's not so bad if she uses the phone once or twice." She seemed to have forgotten that we were on the other end of the line. I was really upset by their brief conversation because it made me more anxious. Unfortunately, I did not have the words to respond so I gave the phone to my sister and told her to tell them we were her daughters and not her friends. Keitumetse took the phone again and found the woman on the other end saying: "Is that all now? Hello? Hello?"

Keitumetse said, "She is my mother. She is not home. Do you know what time she left?"

"She left the same time as usual. I'm sure she'll be home soon, okay? Bye now." Click.

We stood there stunned, Keitumetse still holding the phone. She and I stared at each other in desperation. She held the phone while I held her hand. We were dumbfounded that the woman did not seem to have a clue what we were feeling and that she was not even a little bit concerned. A tear rolled down my sister's cheek and fell on my hand. She could always cry when she felt that bad, but I just never could. I felt heavy all over and held her hand really tightly. We sat down together unsure of what to think. It was almost eleven o'clock and still there was no sign of our mother. I kept going over the voices on the other phone: "Why are you calling at this hour . . . she's not supposed to use the phone." Anger was a little more bearable than worry and fear. "I hate it when they call her that. They don't even know her real name," I said.

"I didn't even remember," Keitumetse said.

"I know. I never think about it. When she leaves here she has one name and when she is at work she has a different name." I tried smiling at my sister, but she was beginning to sob. I had to come up with something else because sitting in the house was only making us both feel a lot more frustrated. After giving it some thought, I suggested to Keitumetse that we go down the street and see if Karabo's mother was there, because the two of them always took the same train.

We decided that I should go since one of us should stay home in case Mama came or someone called. So I hurried down the street towards Karabo's house, constantly looking behind me for signs of my mother and to see that there was no one coming after me. We rarely walked outside after dark, there was too much going on for us to feel safe on the streets at night. So I was running with my eyes darting from side to side, and then I would turn my head back until I was almost running backwards. I ran into a woman, my shoulders crashing into her breasts.

"Aaah!" I shrieked. To my horror, Mma Kleintjie was standing there. I could not have seen her anyway because only one streetlamp was lit and I had been running too fast to see who was on the street. I stood there, my mouth wide open, my heart threatening to burst through my chest, and my throat getting hotter and drier by the second.

"Go back home, you won't find her there," she said.

"Are you everywhere I go?" I spoke out of complete and unguarded anger. As soon as I said it I felt really guilty and apologetic for having spoken that way to someone older.

"I don't want children getting hurt. Don't go outside your home alone at night." She responded without a discernible expression on her face. Either that or it was just too dark to see if she was smiling or frowning. I tried to search her face in the dark. I remembered that last time I had been too afraid to look, so I wanted to remember her that night.

"I'm looking—"

"For your mother, I know. She won't be back for a while. Run back home and someone will tell you what's going on."

My face felt hotter, my limbs got weaker, until I thought I needed something to balance my body before I fell. "Tell me, tell me, please!"

"Tihelo! Tihelo!" Ausi Martha's voice came out from somewhere behind me. "Go home. Go home now. I'm going to get Karabo and we will meet you at your house."

God, Mma Kleintjie is really crazy, I thought to myself as I hurried back home.

Keitumetse was sitting on the *stoep* waiting anxiously. "*Ba re eng*? Did they tell you anything?"

"Ausi Martha said I should come home, she knows something but she's coming with Karabo to tell us."

My sister broke down and sobbed. I stood there trying to say something to make her stop because she was only making me more nervous, but my own mind was racing too fast for me to think straight. I sat down and put my arm around her for a minute, until I had to wrap my arms around myself for comfort. We waited silently together. Of course, we assumed the worst—we knew all too well what could happen to people between the town and the township, or what could happen to workers in White people's homes. Things that no one but the worker would be deemed responsible for. Many neighbours and friends would not return home after work, only to be found in a government mortuary, dead on the road, or alone in hospitals when no one in their families knew where to find them. Women and men would have accidents with electrical appliances or be hit by cars and their "carelessness" would be blamed. We knew that there could have been a train accident. It was not just that anything could have happened, it was that many different horrible things were constantly happening to people every day and we knew that whatever kept my mother from home had to be one of those horrible things. We could only be sure that we had at least one or two nights of distress ahead of us.

✳

I am wearing a dress covered with flowers and shiny black shoes and—although they are itchy—I have agreed to wear a pair of white stockings because my mother says they look so pretty with my shoes and they match my dress. The people she works for are away for two weeks on holiday so Mama is spending two weeks with us. The year before that they thought their child was too small for them to take alone and they took my mother with them so she could care for him. This year they let her stay and she is staying home with me. For my fifth birthday, Mama suggests we go to town and walk around, buy me something special. The town and its large buildings fascinate me. We never do this unless it is a special treat. There are so many people walking, running, it is so busy. I have heard about all the children who have got lost in town, and I cling so tightly to my mother's arm that no one could be strong enough to pull me away from her. Keitumetse is holding on to Mama's other arm, but she is a lot less afraid, she is just enjoying herself. We walk around all day and go into clothing stores just to look, not to buy. The something special that I am getting is not something to wear—I already have a new dress. It will be ice cream or something else to eat. We walk around so much that my feet begin to hurt. The stockings get itchier and I want to stop and have a rest. We walk up to the park and sit down for a while, then I decide it is time for me to eat and my mother says fine, we will go over to that little take-away café and buy some fish and chips. But I protest, I want to sit down somewhere and eat, I don't want to eat on the dirty grass in the park.

My mother says no, that is the only place we will eat. So I throw a tantrum. I yell and scream and scream some more because I am five years old and I think it will make a world of difference and it is the only way to get what I want. My mother says fine, where would I like to eat, and I pull her hand and walk her across the street and into the mall we were walking in before. She says there is probably no place for us to eat in there and I say yes there is, I saw a restaurant with white tablecloths and lots of places to sit and eat. Not only that, but I know it was open because there were people in it. Keitumetse says not to be a baby, but I ignore her. I pull my mother by her arm some more and bring her to the restaurant. We stand outside as I point to it and say there, see, there are people eating in there. The window of the place is so high I have to put my head far back just to see inside. There are people sitting at a table near the window. They are staring at us and we are staring at them. We just stand there staring at each other. A man in a suit comes up to us and says something to my mother and points behind us. My mother brings her whole body down to the same level as mine, holds my arms, and stares straight into my eyes. She says, "See? We are not allowed to go in there."

The police station stank. The very people I constantly feared, the dogs, were roaming around looking and feeling perfectly at home. Keitumetse and I walked in with Ausi Martha and Karabo, all of us holding on really tightly to each other. As if we could all save and

protect one another from the vultures surrounding us. We did not know where to start, where to go. A policeman who looked like the person we were supposed to be talking to was surrounded by many people waiting to ask him all kinds of questions. Families had come in taxis from the townships in the middle of the night to ask for their mothers and fathers who had never made it home after work that evening. Who was to say if we even had any chance of finding our parents there? Who was to say if the dogs would account for them?

All the way to the station I kept wondering: What if they just say they cannot tell us who was and who was not there when they got to the station? They could definitely say that. The more I thought about it, the more I convinced myself that was exactly what they would say. The whole way there I was preparing myself for the worst. I thought it would make sense: the police raided the Blacks-only train station and found many women and men either without passes or without train tickets. Passes were the only form of identification they considered valid, and if you did not carry one, how could you prove that the person you were looking for had been there to begin with? If my mother had disappeared, I thought, it would take forever for us to find her, or any other place that would take the time to let us know they had found her. I kept picturing the missing persons reports after the seven o'clock news where they would have drawings of faces of bodies they found just about everywhere in the country. People would see long-lost uncles and cousins on that television show. My sister and I always covered our eyes because the pictures were always so terrifying, I thought they made the people look grotesque. Mama always said, "You know, once there was a family that hid their eyes whenever a particularly scary police sketch of a person came on, and one day they missed a picture of someone who was related to them."

It was always this big joke around the house. We watched that show all the time, but Keitumetse and I only ever saw about one out of every four of those faces. That night it did not seem so funny. I kept wondering if I was going to have to identify my mother.

I was barely able to walk that crisp April night when we entered the police station. The people who were standing and waiting for answers may as well have had no one to speak to. The policemen stood around drinking their coffee and telling jokes to each other as if there was no one else around. We must have been there for a whole hour before we got any form of attention from the police, and that was to tell us to keep it down. The place was overcrowded with desperate masses, groups of angry people who knew better than to express their frustration in any way in that room. So while we were all seething, people were as polite as they had learned to be around those uniforms.

However, as always, strangers were speaking to each other, trying to make sense of what was going on. As the night dragged on, this was pretty much what people understood: Men and women returning from work were rushing into the station to catch the six-thirty train when green uniforms burst into the place, stopping everyone and demanding they show their passes. Some people, my mother included, thought this was the police's way of telling them to hurry up and leave a White area because Black people were not allowed there after dark. They thought that maybe they could get away if they caught the train and rode away. So they started running onto the platform but never made their way into the carriages. A few hundred men and women were beaten with batons, whips, and the back ends of the long guns just because they had run. People were shocked as to why the police would not have let the people go since they were about to leave town anyway.

They were all illegal immigrants in their own country. Every morning they would travel about an hour away to be in a different country, on different territory, and they would have to carry the right papers to show that they were not illegally crossing borders, looking for work in what another man had declared his own land. Many of our parents worked in areas that used to be their own, places previously owned by their grandparents, neighbourhoods their mothers had grown up in. All that time, they had to show proof that they had the right to be there, to walk and work in homes

situated where their mothers and fathers were once woken up in the middle of the night and moved out at gunpoint.

I remember wondering if my mother had even been given the time to show her pass, I knew she had recently renewed it. Someone who must have been thinking the same thing asked if it mattered whether or not you had a pass, to which someone else answered that that was not entirely the point. The police had a mission—they needed to torture and harass people into fearing them, plus they hated seeing people run and get away. This just aggravated them. As if there was ever anything we did that had the opposite effect. We huddled in that room for hours, fear turning into exhaustion. Some of us fell asleep on top of each other. I had rested my head on Ausi Martha's lap and was about to drift into sleep when a noise broke out. People were screaming and cursing, apparently having got sick and tired of the wait and less afraid of the guns. My eyes were barely open when I hastily followed the crowd outside, the police leading us out with their guns pointed at our heads, telling us we could wait outside in the cold. We stood and waited for a while in the cold, unsure of whether or not we would go home with the people we had come for.

It was dawn when they came walking out. I often prefer not to remember seeing our people in that space, all bruised and their clothes torn like that. They looked humiliated and afraid. My eyes met my mother's with difficulty. She was pulling her shirt together with one hand and covering her left eye with another. Her shirt was torn at her breasts and ripped in the back in long neat stripes, and her eye was about three different colours. When she approached me, I was torn between staring at her and pretending I did not notice. It was unnerving, seeing my mother's bra exposed in public. I averted my eyes out of respect. Keitumetse just ran and hugged her. People were crying at the sight of their relatives. Women who had come to take their sisters home were breaking down, carrying their hands on their heads like heavy burdens. Sisters were afraid of the humiliation in their brothers' faces. Children were cringing at the sight of their scarred and bruised fathers with blood on their clothes. It had been an excruciatingly long night. One man's forehead had been bleeding all night and he had taken off his shirt, using it to stop the bleeding. He was dizzy and weak and someone was holding him, supporting him. I thought to myself, At least he doesn't have to see the looks on his children's faces.

At least they were alive and we did not have to go and identify them in some government mortuary.

The next day the news was all over the township. People were coming and going every few minutes at our house, wanting to know how Mama was doing. Karabo's mother had not been hit as badly, so she came and sat with us that evening after work. People had got up and gone to work as if they had no wounds to care for. They would have risked losing their jobs if they had stayed home and taken care of themselves, so they picked themselves up and fell back into their everyday routine, going right back to the scene of the trauma. But Mama could not have gone back that soon even though she needed to. We found that she was more hurt than she had thought on the first night. Her back was cut open from the whip and the wounds burned an awful lot.

Every day the sun would come and go, finding and leaving Mama in the same place. She just sat and stared out, like someone fascinated by the change of seasons. Maybe she was taking everything in really slowly for the first time in her life. Maybe she was just lying there contemplating her future. She never said more than two words all that week. Neighbours who came in bringing their good wishes were stunned at how she seemed to be so far away, sometimes even unaware of what was going on around her. She slept and woke up in the same spot, never lifting a finger—a sure sign that something was terribly wrong, if anyone yet noticed. My sister and I sat in bed with her, we read her the newspaper and brought her food, which she just poked at with her spoon for a moment without ever really eating anything. She would drink tea and water, but ate nothing. At night she would scream and wake us, but when we came for her she pretended to be asleep so that we would not attempt to comfort her.

Here I was, fourteen years old and feeling like the adult of the house. Keitumetse just wrapped herself around our mother, seeking comfort. She would come home from school and tell her about her whole day, not really caring if she got any response, just satisfied to have Mama there. In all families people take on different roles when going through hard times, and mine was that of the caregiver. I cleaned, cooked, did the washing, and never attempted to get words out of my mother. I was afraid of that thing that was living within her, consuming the parts of her that I was most familiar with. She made me uncomfortable, this other woman. Sometimes I could have sworn her eyes were watering and I could not bear to look. That was the third time that I had seen my mother cry. Taking care of everything was my way of walking away from my discomfort with this new woman in the house. I thought my mother was humiliated, I thought she was also afraid, and neither one of those were demons I had ever been brave enough to face. I tiptoed around them constantly, taking command from them, letting them make me their puppet, and taking care not to collide with them. I would look in any direction as long as it was away from them.

We grow up watching our mothers slide through distress, and that is how we are able to face it ourselves. When I was a little girl I would cry from physical pain because my mother would never cry from her own physical pain, and because she would easily take care of mine. It is only when our mothers can handle what we fear that it is possible for us to face it head on. They are our best protection against it. I could have never faced my fear and humiliation if I had allowed myself to watch my mother be consumed by her own.

8

MOHAU RETURNED BOLDLY from the underground world at the beginning of May. I found out by seeing him one morning at the SASO headquarters when I went in with Tshepo. My sister, who I thought I had left at home sleeping, was in fact curled at his side on the couch in the part of the office that would have been a living room if it were a house. But I was more stunned at the sight of her boyfriend. He was skinny, very skinny, with a beard and dreadlocks. His skin had lost quite a bit of colour, which led me to imagine the underground world as some place that was actually situated underground. He looked like he had not seen the sun in years.

He looked up at me and said, very softly, like he thought he was speaking to his biggest fan: "Hello, comrade. How have you been?"

"Fine," I responded cooly, and then continued, "Tshepo, let's start working."

Tshepo of course wanted nothing to do with T-shirts or fliers or anything like that. He just wanted to sit and speak to his brother.

"I'll go and work alone then," I said and went to the room we usually worked in with my slice of bread and peanut butter.

Everyone seemed to gather around Mohau and listen to him talk about his underground stories.

"I have to stay quiet," he was saying, "just in case."

I was sitting in that room pretending to work, resenting every minute of being at the office. I thought, Doesn't he realize that he is taking pride in being a part of something that has created such turmoil? All the riots and marches were draining to me. At this point I felt no strong connection with the comrades, even if I was working with them daily. Instead, I resented their zeal. I even sometimes blamed them for being so forceful and determined because I thought that if they were a little more calm then the township might have been less chaotic. It no longer made any difference whether it was Saturday or Monday. People, particularly high-school students, had stopped going to school and thinking of it as a regular and necessary step in their lives. I would walk past Karabo's house after school, and she would be sweeping her yard. It was as if she had not even planned to go to school. When I asked, she would say, "Maybe I'll go tomorrow." Maybe. There was so much despair. I did not want to be part of the organizing, making fliers or being there at all. Being at the headquarters was not becoming any easier, and it was increasingly difficult for me to feel like we were making any progress. Everything, every event, protest, or boycott, took such a toll on us. We would lose students and comrades to the police every time, and writing about it was really hard for me.

How could Mohau see anything to be proud of in that? Was it a macho, manly thing that drove him to want to be at the forefront of riots and demonstrations? We were accomplishing nothing in my opinion, but he spoke with so much hope and no fear whatsoever. Tshepo called me into the next room to come and hear something, a story about how his brave brother was a survivor, and I took my cue. I stomped in there and said, "I do not want to work here anymore," and started heading for the door. Everyone stared and I ignored their eyes and looked straight ahead.

Dikeledi stood behind me and said, "Thank you, comrade," which made me stand still and stare at the wall in front of me. My body was being weighed down by that heavy feeling again. "You have been such a big help. You know, we could do the fliers and the newsletters, we could even paint the shirts. But we feel strongly about all youths being part of this, because we are all living the same crisis, you know? You have been a loyal and faithful comrade, and you are brave. We will miss you." She ended with the Setswana greeting, "*Tsamaya ka kagiso.* Go in peace."

I did not feel like she was begging me to stay, her gesture did not feel manipulative at all. It felt honest and heartfelt. She was wishing me the best, and I appreciated it very much. I warmed up to her a little. And more than anything, it felt satisfying to be thanked formally, officially. It was as if she had given me a ticket to leave. I felt that at that point, I had a choice and no one was pushing me in either direction. I could have done this months ago, I thought to myself. Although I had not felt completely comfortable there, I had enjoyed what I had been doing. It made me proud to see my writing on fliers and working to meet deadlines was exhilarating. In there, my desire to be a journalist felt real, tangible. But it was time for me to go. I had just been moving from day to day, unaware of anything apart from my terror and my melancholy for so long, and sometimes I thought that if I could just cry I would feel a lot less heavy. But tears did not come so easily to me.

Keitumetse came running after me down the street. I stopped and waited for her to reach me, preparing myself for defence.

"You should stay," she said, breathless. "People really like you there, you should stay. If you want I can start working there with you. If it will make you feel safer."

"*Ha-e,*" I said. "No."

"Why not?" she demanded. "It's very secure. No one has found it, have they? And you've been there about five months now."

"I'm too tired," I said, listless. "I need to just stay home and rest."

"You are not going to school now?"

"*Ha-e.*"

I just walked aimlessly for a while. Going around and around the township, thinking. I would pass green vans speeding past me, leaving me covered in dust. When I was in middle school, there had been a rule that no schoolchildren in uniform were allowed to be on the streets in the middle of the day. If the police found you walking around, you would be picked up and taken to school. No one thought anything of me walking the streets in my school uniform. I was only one of hundreds of students on the streets. Teachers would sit in their staff rooms for hours speaking to each other, rarely taking the time to teach. We were really going to school to meet our friends and chat. There was no other reason to go every morning.

Mohau's grandfather was sitting at his usual spot under the mupudu tree in the front yard, moving with the shade as the day moved on.

"*Dumelang*," I greeted him respectfully.

"*Agé*, Tihelo," he responded "*Tlaa kwano*. Come here."

I walked over and stood on the outside, holding on to the fence.

"Mama *hao*, how is she?"

"She is fine, I think she is a lot better," I responded, fully aware that I had not asked my mother how she had been feeling in weeks, inwardly upset by my neglect.

"I see she is walking around the yard today. That's good, she must come out and see the sun."

My mother outside? She had not even been to the kitchen since we came home from the police station. I pretended I knew all about it, said it was really good to see her getting up and moving, and leaped into our yard immediately.

She was sitting on the back *stoep*, all washed up and wearing a clean cotton dress instead of her nightgown. With her long regal body erect and a pensive rather than a gloomy look on her face, there was a familiar grace about her. A plate of food rested on her lap and she was chewing away, watching the blossoming mupudu tree, its fruit still green and hard. She turned and looked straight at me, right into my eyes, as I walked in. She did not say a word. I looked right back at her, feeling that I owed her that much. I sat next to her and for a while we watched the mupudu tree in silence.

She reached out her hand with the plate of food in it and I moulded a piece of *bogobe*, wrapping the gravy and the dried spinach around it with my fingers. We ate together for a few minutes without saying anything. She just kept looking around the yard at the bare peach trees and back at the blossoming mupudu. I had not really looked at her for so long. I had nothing to say to her, really, I just felt alone and angry with her for not getting up sooner and fighting back. I was angry with her for letting this other weaker and less protective woman enter our lives. Maybe I found it easier to let myself feel that anger because it was easier to face the person I was sitting next to than it had been to visit the other woman in my mother's bed all those weeks.

"How is work at the headquarters?" she asked, turning to look at me.

"I . . ."

"What? Five months and you think I had no idea?"

"I'm not working there anymore. I stopped today," I said, apologetically.

"Good. You don't need it anymore."

"What do you mean? There is still so much work to be done at the office, and so much less to go to school for."

"I go back to work tomorrow," she said, ignoring my question. Then, turning and looking back at the tree, she added: "I expect you and your sister to be back in school."

The following day my mother got up before I did and returned at six o'clock in the evening with a new job. This time she worked in a take-away café owned by a Greek man with a temper a lot gentler than anyone she had had to answer to before. He sold cooked food and junk food as well as fruits and vegetables in his store, employing a few black men and women to work in the kitchen, his daughters and wife at the till, and my mother cleaning both the produce and the store. She said she liked it somewhat better because she did not have to be there on Sundays. Also, at lunchtime many men and women who worked in town came to the shop to buy bread with *atchar* and chips, and *bogobe* with meat. Seeing people from the township made her feel somewhat more secure in town.

*

Mma Modise is the most faithful churchgoer you will ever meet. Every Sunday morning at seven o'clock sharp she is standing in the front row of the big sunny church they built from five years of fundraising, singing from the bottom of her heart. Ask her any day how she is and you are guaranteed to hear about the grace of God, the power of our Lord, the all-knowing and all-powerful protector. She believes in the force of one God more than she believes in anything or anyone else, and she gives her life to the teachings of the Catholic church that stands towering above all houses on the other side of the main road.

She also gives her Sunday afternoons over to teaching Sunday school to the children of the Catholic parents of our township, and she devotes her Saturday mornings to cleaning the inside of the house of her Lord. Every Sunday evening when she returns from spending the whole afternoon in church, she stops by my house to see if my sister and I are doing well. We make her tea and she sits in our kitchen telling us about the wonders of her God, how he always provides.

My mother does not like her one bit, but she is very polite when she arrives home every Sunday evening and finds Mma Modise sitting at her kitchen table, talking to her two daughters about how they should give their lives to the Lord. My mother always greets her with a regret, that only we can detect in her voice. She is always asking us to make up stories and tell Mma Modise that she will probably not be home that evening. We might have to say that she has been asked by her missies to stay overnight because they need her. Sometimes my mother even tells us to pretend we are not home and not open the door for her. We never do that because if she does not find us the first time she will return again and again. Until she knows that my mother will be returning soon enough, at which point she sits and waits at our doorstep, and when my mother arrives we pretend we have been sleeping. It does not work well for my sister and I because then we have to be quiet for a long time pretending that no one is home. So we tell my mother to think of something else if she wants to keep Mma Modise away from our house.

At weddings, when elders begin to praise and lecture the newlyweds about family and ancestors and love between a man and a woman, Mma Modise praises God. She is the chief mourner at every funeral, crying the loudest and the hardest. She has told my sister and me that if she were not Catholic then she would probably be looking forward to becoming a priest and someday maybe even a bishop. There is no greater joy than the joy of serving the Lord our God, she tells us. I am in primary school and Keitumetse is in middle school, both of us have religion classes and we hear what she is saying all week, but never with as much passion. She is a true believer, my mother sometimes tells us when Mma Modise decides to leave, usually after her tenth cup of tea. We are often running out of milk and sugar by the time she leaves. But she has the kind of faith that you only hear about in books, my mother says. A true believer.

At Christmas her brother comes home from Gauteng driving the fanciest car anyone has ever seen. He hit the jackpot by placing bets on racehorses, he tells everyone. Soon every boy in the township is running around him like he is a hero. They smell and touch the car and offer to wash it for him every five minutes. He loves the attention, and gives the boys money for cleaning the car. He tells them about how someday they too will be where he is. "Just you wait, mfana," *he says to his fan of the day. "If you are smart and you know how to survive, you will live the life I am living some day." All the boys swoon and keep running and playing in those places in their imaginations where they are already living that life. Then one day he throws a party for the neighbourhood, celebrating his money, and announces that he is going to build a house for his sister because she has taken care of him all his life.*

After New Year's Day he climbs into the car of our dreams and rides off to the world of our imaginations. The next day at dawn Mma Modise kneels in her backyard, digs a hole in the ground, and holds a bowl full of ash in one hand, and another bowl full of water in the other hand. She pours the ash into the hole, drinks the water, and spits it into the hole, all the time bowing her head and looking up to the sky, praying and thanking the ancestors for her good fortune.

9

AT SEVENTEEN, MY sister knew she had done nothing different from most other women in the township when she woke up one morning vomiting her colourful, smelly guilt and fear into the toilet, her dreams disappearing with the subsequent swirl of water. She watched herself fearfully, silently, until one day she decided to look herself straight in the eye. She went to see the doctor, who informed her that there was nothing to be afraid of, and that she was "only" going to have a child. After it was too heavy for her to carry alone, she decided to tell me about it. She had been sobbing on her pillow when she woke me, right after Mama had left the house. I listened to her as she kept swearing that she had "only done it once," and not understanding what could have happened.

"It's not like I'm a *sekhebereshe*," she said. "We only did it once when Mohau first came back."

We were both stunned. How could we not be? We had been brought up to believe that this only happened to other girls—those who spent no time at home and who slept with many different men. Even though we knew that our mother had had a child when she was young, we never thought of her that way because she also talked about this as something that only happened to other people. She had never actually told either one of us that she had had a child just before she went off to nursing school, my sister had just overheard it when we were younger. This was the kind of truth that was so secret that we forgot it was real.

Keitumetse's first thought was that she should tell Mohau. I thought he should never hear a word about it. I tried to convince my

71

sister to think about her future, about actually not having the baby and doing something else with it. But I could not have been less convincing if I tried, as the thought of an abortion terrified me. I had heard all kinds of stories about how women had been hurt, traumatized, and even killed from terminating their pregnancies. Abortion fell under the unknown illness category in the list of explanations for women's deaths, another thing my sister had explained to me years before. She kept saying that if she terminated the pregnancy then she would not be able to have children ever again. We never heard about how women had abortions, but only about how, when they did, they were never able to have children again because abortions were so unsafe. It was another fear-instilling survival tactic—if we were going to leave and make our lives better we had to fear the things that could force us to stay. If we thought abortion killed, we would not have unwanted pregnancies, and if we wanted to avoid pregnancies then we would avoid sex.

Abortion was never spoken of with kind words, and my sister was determined not to do something that was considered abominable by both the men and women around her. But most of all she was terrified of telling my mother. Frankly, so was I. Mama would be afraid for us, and that would most probably manifest itself as pure and utter rage.

The day was just drifting by and we took no notice. My sister was trying to recover from the shock of her life. Our neighbour had had an all-night *gazi*—a party where people sold beer out of their house to their guests, and a very popular way of making money—so we woke up to the same music that had been playing the night before when we had gone to sleep. It was almost late afternoon and neither one of us had done any cleaning, we were still in our nightgowns trying to decide how to tell Mama. Soon we would have to make sure that the house was clean before Mama came back, so we pulled ourselves together and started to dust and sweep, both of us in a daze. We spoke as we cleaned, trying to decide on ways of telling both Mama and Mohau. I was doubtful that he would take the news well, he just seemed very self-absorbed, acted like a know-it-all. My heart leaped every time I pictured my sister telling him. I was too weary of the outcome. Either he would do the manly thing and want to get married and find a job, or he would completely abandon my sister. Both ideas made me feel uneasy.

By the time the sun set, I had already decided that I had to be by my sister's side when she told her boyfriend. I was also planning what we would do if he wanted nothing to do with the pregnancy. I could see him saying the child was not his. I could see him flat out denying he had anything to do with all that. It would be easy too, because he had not been around very often and could easily deny responsibility to his grandparents. By the time I was finished doing my part of the cleaning, I could not decide if I had been thinking all that because I really believed that Mohau was so irresponsible, or if I was just feeling regretful about my sister losing her chance to leave the township. Maybe I secretly wanted him to deny everything so that Keitumetse would not want to have a baby. It seemed unfair that so many young women were confined to a life of despair simply because they made mistakes they did not even know how to avoid. In the mid-eighties, having a baby before you finished school meant letting go of everything you had hoped for, leaving behind those bigger and better places that you had imagined for as long as you could remember. Yet there was no way we could have known how not to fall into the trap. Mothers valued the wide gap between generations, saw it as something that kept our respect for them strong. They could not see themselves sitting and talking to us about intimate relationships because, to them, that meant acknowledging that we had those kinds of feelings, and they felt that admitting it would only make us more comfortable with our sexuality. And that, they thought, could only encourage us to have sex.

My sister's pregnancy only increased my own fear. I could not believe this was happening in our house. It made me feel more stuck, magnified the feeling of being trapped forever in the township. As was my nature, I desperately wanted to find ways to care for her. I was walking around frantically trying to find a way to make it all good and perfect before my mother suspected anything. I wanted to speak with someone I trusted. I could not tell Ausi Martha because she would tell the whole neighbourhood, and I could not tell any of my friends without feeling like I was betraying my sister's confidence. But I had to keep thinking, because I was not leaving my sister here in the *lekeishene*. For the next few days I walked around in a daze, trying to make a plan.

In school, Lebo was cheerful and funny, which made me feel like I had imagined the incident at her house. She and I would come in every morning with about two books in our schoolbags, which we only carried because it made us look like we were going in to learn something. I was aware of her embarrassment, I knew she so badly hoped that I would not say a word about her father. It was not hard to tell that she felt so embarrassed about me having noticed her father's missing arm, that she did not care so much if I had seen how angry he was and how much he terrified her. Somehow the latter was more tolerable to a lot of women, we did not feel like it was unusual because men were always angry and throwing fits of frustration all around us.

We would sit in class talking, sharing gossip and stories about her dancing. Every once in a while a teacher would come in and sit at his or her desk, tell us to turn our textbooks to a certain page because they had woken up that morning and decided they would spend some time teaching that day. Inevitably, not only would half the class not be present, but almost none of us would have the right books. This would fuel the teacher's fury, and they would stand up and tell us what hopeless cases we all were, how we thought riots would get us somewhere but how they were only a waste of our time. Sometimes they would decide that we were so bad and so frustrating that it was time to beat us into the intelligent, school-loving children they were hoping to find in class that day. Some students had taken to talking back and telling the teacher exactly what to do with those words. Sometimes a teacher would be targeted as *mpimpi*. Initially meaning a spy, the word now meant a worthless government scum who had nothing better to do with their time than to harass students. Occasionally a teacher would be asked by students to choose their words wisely if they did not want to see their car or home petrol-bombed to the ground.

Any previous reverence we had had for teachers before entering high school had disappeared with our escalating frustration. No one thought authority was worth any respect. Students had come to see anyone in a position of power as useless and unintelligent. We thought we knew everything, the way all teenagers do, except that we were living under circumstances that made that feeling very dangerous. Adolescents in high school were losing their desire to listen to those who had absolute power to wreck our lives. The police were detaining and killing students, and the teachers were only sharing about an ounce of their knowledge each week. We felt extremely angry with everyone. Even our parents were not protecting us. The days of mothers and fathers going into school and speaking to the teachers about their concerns were long gone. We were having so many stay-aways that the parents themselves would not have had much of a case to argue on our behalf. So we just grew into hopelessness because we were constantly running and hiding from danger. I watched in horror as students vandalized people's property, making it look as though we were in control when in fact we were terrified.

On one of those lazy days when no teacher paid us a visit—when we decided what time we came in and when we went to lunch—Lebo and I went walking the streets with other groups of students. All of us were either on our way to the shops to buy lunch or just strolling around the township for hours. I had decided that maybe I would bring up my sister's pregnancy with Lebo and make it look as if I was speaking of someone else. I told her about this girl, a very distant cousin of mine whom she had never met. This "cousin" was pregnant and thinking of not having the baby. I had already decided in my mind that Keitumetse was not having the baby and that I was supposed to try and help her find a way to get rid of her very big problem. Lebo was very casual and unconcerned about this cousin.

She was a very nonjudgmental person, which was unusual around here and made it easier for me open up even more.

"I heard you can use Javel or Dettol. You drink it, and the baby just comes out," she told me.

"But isn't that poison?" I asked.

"That's why it works, it stops the baby from fully forming, just kills it."

When I look back on that conversation now and remember us speaking about abortion in that grossly misinformed way, it makes me cringe. We knew so little, dangerously little.

"I also heard that if you fall on your stomach it can kill the baby," she continued. I flinched.

"What else? Do you know of a doctor who will do it?"

"No! Don't go to a doctor, tell her to do it fast and cheap. All by herself. Women have been doing abortions on themselves for so long. Everyone around here does it. I wouldn't be in school if I didn't believe in abortion."

I was surprised that she told me so easily. I would never have been able to say that out loud. I would never have told anyone if I had had an abortion. But it always made me more comfortable to see a woman dismiss her own shame. It made me feel at ease with Lebo; I liked some of who she was a lot.

"How did you do it?" I asked softly, reluctant to pry.

"Is it you?"

"Me what?"

"Who is pregnant. Is it you?"

"Oh, no! It's my cousin, I told you."

"Why are you so concerned then? She is not so close to you is she? I mean, you never talk about her so—"

"She calls sometimes. She called my sister and me because she thinks we know everything. She doesn't have sisters so she always asks us when she needs some advice. I worry about her."

"Okay. Hmm, let me see. The first time I just bled, but I didn't know how that happened because I hadn't used anything. The second time I used a wire."

She said it so casually that I thought she was joking. I tried to look unfazed, I needed to look mature and casual.

"That must have hurt," I said.

"I ended up in the hospital for a few days. The nurses called me *sekhebereshe*, but that was the least of my problems. What have they done for me anyway, right? Who needs them?"

I paused awhile, taking in deep breaths. Eventually I asked, "Did your father know?"

We were both silent for a minute or two. I stared at the students in black and white, their numbers increasing on the streets. I thought of going back to class and reading something. Maybe we could both go back, I thought. The conversation had been uncomfortable, and I almost regretted asking the last question because it seemed like the hardest for Lebo to answer. Somehow the carefree attitude she had had before was suddenly gone. She did not look at me when she said, softly, "He knows."

I did not want my sister's dilemma to become to a big neighbourhood scandal where, by the time Mama had the customary meeting with Mohau's grandparents, everyone around us would already be gossiping about it. I feared my mother's anger and was mortified for my sister. People were watching, and in my family I was always the one acutely aware of the neighbourhood's gaze. I cared the most about their opinions. At home Keitumetse and I spoke about it when Mama was at work. Keitumetse would spent a lot of time away from her, pretending to be studying whenever Mama was home. I was back to sleeping before Mama arrived home in the evenings because I continued to feel less and less hopeful about what would happen to me. We were in the middle of the year, the winter holidays approaching, and there was not even talk of half-year exams. The Black newspapers were reporting doom with headlines like "50% fail expected in matriculants" and "Students planning to stay away from exams." It only made us feel like there was no one out there who had any kind of faith in us, which in turn made it harder to see going to school as worthwhile.

I tried all the time to remember what Mama always said, that if we did not fight we would agree to stay here forever. Sometimes it made me feel better, but other times it seemed pointless. Riots still made me angry. Selfishly, I wanted to be in class learning something, halfway to the exhilarating life of a journalist. I still allowed myself some time to pack up my belongings and go live in my future, that very invigorating place in my imagination that was most comfortable. I had to keep thinking it still existed and I relied on it desperately, because my fears never went into my imagination with me, they never even appeared. Lately I had been looking to find my sister in there also, because I refused to believe she could not or would not come. She would be a nurse like she had wanted to, and all that we had discussed together would still happen. It would just be a little while longer, I told myself. We just had to move through this part of things.

But Keitumetse told Mohau. I was not there like I had wanted to be, and she went ahead and told him anyway, which made me feel as though I was not as much a part of her decision making as I would have liked. Mohau, to my surprise, talked about how he would provide for her and the baby, about how he would be a father to his son. Already he had decided that was the sex of the baby. Keitumetse said that at the offices she felt out of place, as if she had changed the course of a revolution. Without straight out saying so, some of the boys felt that they needed Mohau and that he should not be thinking about going to work in town labouring away at the command of White men. He needed to stay right there and work for his people. On the other hand, the women empathized, some of them telling her in strict confidence that they had been in the same situation.

I was very angry and anxious about his decision, because I got the sense that it made Keitumetse feel like she had some kind of permission to be pregnant. Although still afraid, she felt somewhat less anxious. It was something I really did not like about Keitumetse, her need to check with everyone on everything that concerned her. Her plans and decisions often depended on Mama's or her friends' approval.

She needed someone else to approve of what she was about to do. My plan for her to terminate the pregnancy seemed to be out of the question because her boyfriend approved of her having a baby, and he saw his girlfriend's pregnancy as an affirmation of his manhood. He bragged about having a child, even though he was still a whole year away from finishing high school.

"No, Tihelo," she would say to me. "I don't want that. It's dangerous, and Mama would be very angry with me. Besides, Mohau has no problem with it."

"But he doesn't have to have a problem with it. What about you? You had a problem with it a few days ago, you couldn't have changed your mind just because he is happy with it."

"But it will be okay. I can still go to nursing school. Mama and his grandmother will take care of the baby."

"Keitumetse, Mama will not stop working just to stay home and take care of your baby. You know that. Mohau's grandmother might, but Mama would never let you do that, she will make you take full responsibility."

We had a lot of really long nights those first few days, whispering together in our bedroom so that Mama would not hear us. I persisted in trying to convince my sister not to hold on to things that would steal away her future. She thought I was too young to understand and spoke to me like I was an annoying little girl, but I was still convinced that she had a lot of the same doubts and was just as apprehensive as I was. She would not admit it to me because she needed to convince herself that what was happening was not as big as I made it out to be. She needed to believe that the little girl in her was still alive, that she would walk right through this predicament and come out unscathed.

On television there are shows that promise to make you feel like a star for a night. If you have a talent, and if, when you dream, you can see yourself capturing the attention of people all around you with that talent, you can apply to be on Dinaledi (Stars), the most popular talent

*show on TV3. You will be famous for about a week after that, and peo-
ple will recognize you because there isn't a single person in the township
who does not manage to be near a television on Friday night just to
watch that show. And it is not just your township, but every township
where people watch TV3.*

*So, stardom being as attractive as anything that makes you feel very
important, a group of us from the same street come together in Thato's
backyard to practise a dance that we put together. We are preparing for
our night of stardom. A group of judges comes around to a different
township every week and we have heard that soon they will be in our
neighbourhood. Auditions are very hard, we hear. It is quite competi-
tive. We work dilligently every day after school. We are at Thato's house
for hours until sunset, practising to take TV3 viewers by storm. Every
day we imagine and dream, imagine and dream. Our legs are covered
in dust from dancing in the unpaved backyard. The dust rises and sticks
to the grease of Vaseline that we cover our legs with every morning before we go to school to avoid excessive drying.*

*Any day now those judges will be coming around to look at our
moves, to be dazzled by our collective talent. On the weekends a
woman drives up and down the streets in a little car with a large loudspeaker calling on women and children to come and join her at the
shops for a dance competition. There are prizes to be won, a show to
watch. So we all run there excitedly. The women are hoping to win the
washing powder and the children are hoping to win a few rand.*

*So here we are, half the township in a small tight space in the yard of
the general store, having the time of our lives. The mothers go first. The
woman from the small car with the loudspeaker stands there asking
questions about our president, our national anthem, and our lives here.
So every woman gives it her best, and someone ends up going home
with a few months' supply of washing powder. Next it is the children.
We all start dancing. There are so many of us you wonder how we are
all able to do it in such a small space. But we are just hoping someone
notices and is absolutely taken by our skill. We keep going and going
and the woman on the loudspeaker keeps stopping the music, telling us*

who stays and who goes. In the end only three people are left and one of them will be the winner. My friend Peter is one of the last dancers, and we are not surprised. He is breakdancing like those American youths you see in brightly coloured clothes on TV, dancing in dance halls. He is covered in dust, but he is in his element and we are all loving it. Finally they announce the winner and it is Peter. He is a star. He has always known it but now everyone else does too: he has potential.

Keitumetse was sitting in her room one evening when my mother came home and decided we had to have a family conference. She woke me up from about two hours of sleep and said it was urgent enough that we had to be awakened. All three of us went into her room and sat on her bed, my sister and I feeling uneasy because Mama looked so distraught. Her window was open and a cold wind was blowing in. Sometimes Mama liked to come home and sit facing the window, letting the breeze come in and blow away the day's fatigue. On that day she sat there staring, looking like she had a lot to speak to us about. I was really apprehensive because of the look on Mama's face. Last time we had had a family meeting Keitumetse and I were barred from playing on the streets and had to stay home selling ice-pops. It was one of those times when I felt that whatever Mama had to say, I did not want to be there to hear it.

But she was determined for me to hear it. She did not say a word for what seemed like much a long time, as if she was letting us all settle down before she spoke. Then she began slowly, her voice low and firm.

"Keitumetse, does Mohau know about that child you are carrying?" My sister looked unfazed. Either she was too tired to try a lie, or she was relieved that it was all out in the open. I, on the other hand, wanted the earth to open up and swallow me.

Mama looked at me sternly and said, "Tihelo, you cannot fix everyone's problems. Keep an eye on your own concerns for a while, you don't need to add our loads on your back."

"Mama," Keitumetse started. "I didn't know."

"You didn't know what? That I wouldn't find out or that sleeping with a boy would get you here?"

"I didn't know I would get pregnant," she responded feebly.

I think my mother did not respond because of her own guilt, but this was not the time to admit it. I watched uncomfortably as her expression shifted from stern to sadness.

"I want to make one thing clear. Womanhood is not for girls with dreams. It is for those of us who forget what we dream of." Sometimes older women said "womanhood" as if it was synonymous with "struggle," like it was one of life's greatest challenges, and that you could only face it when you were ready. When I heard the word I would sometimes cringe and feel apprehensive about getting older. They made it sound like nothing could be harder.

"I really don't want you to feel as if you have to give into something that you had no way of avoiding," Mama continued, turning to look Keitumetse straight in the eye. "You didn't choose this, it was a mistake, and you don't have to live with it in any way that interferes with who you want to be. What do you want to do?"

We both sat there staring out the window, my sister and I shivering because of the chilly breeze that blew in, my mother calmly letting it hit her bare arms. I think neither of us knew exactly what she was saying. I thought she was suggesting an abortion, but that was just what my hope speaking.

"Nothing. I want to have the baby." Keitumetse sounded as though she had resigned herself to it instead of having made a decision she was pleased with.

"Okay . . . then this boy should take full responsibility. Just because you are a woman does not mean you have to stay home and take care of the baby on your own. It means you have to share duties fully. I'm not having my child stay home because she had a baby. You will make sure that if anyone stays home to care for the baby, it's not you. Let him find some time to babysit. There won't be any going to Gauteng or Pretoria, he will be as much of a father as you will be a mother because you did this together. No one told us this when we were young, that we did not have to give up on our own hopes and watch men walk away from responsibility."

I was partly horrified and relieved. Horrified because Mama was giving Keitumetse permission to have a baby, and relieved because she did not fume. God! I thought, I really resent that boy. What did Keitumetse see in him anyway? I had no patience for his national-hero status around here. It made me think that it was that much harder for my sister to think straight about him. What on earth did she have with him that made her willing to stay here? At that point I thought I would never understand.

Keitumetse wrapped herself around Mama as if she was two years old again. It was strange how there was not even a hint of anger in my mother's voice—I was so sure she would think it unforgivable. I was wrong, she thought it would be more sensible to be supportive. For me, it was not the best reaction. I wanted Mama to tell Keitumetse that there were alternatives to having a baby.

Someone I did not know, a neighbour's sister, was getting married that weekend. Why they would have thought to have a wedding in the winter was a mystery to me, but celebrations were always a good idea. The wedding would take place on Saturday at the groom's house and on Sunday at the bride's house. Mapitse, Peter's mother and the person related to this bride, was having the wedding at her house. She put up a white flag at her gate, a way of letting the town-ship know there would be a wedding celebration. As soon as the flag went up, the women and men of the neighbourhood went over there to see what they could do to help with the preparations. In the eve-nings, even though my mother was exhausted, she fulfilled her neighbourly duty by going over to help the other women bake cookies and peel vegetables for cooking. The elders were there every day too. Whoever was not working would be there in the morning making tea for the ageing women who sat on the floor in the bed-rooms as a way of giving their blessings to the bride.

We anticipated a big and exhilarating event. Peter's relatives were coming from every township in South Africa to celebrate. We had even heard that the woman getting married worked for White people who liked her so much that she had invited them. Most of us could hardly wait to see White people right here in the township, dancing and singing with us on the same street. Mma Pitse went around bragging about how her sister worked for what she called really good White people, and about how they were coming to her very own house on Sunday. People were curious and some were even jealous that someone—one of us—was going to have the privilege of having White people in her home. Mma Pitse was stressed out trying to decide how she could make them feel most comfortable in her two-room.

Meanwhile, I was still trying to find a way to get my sister to change her mind about having a baby, but I had not thought of anything yet. I was trying to look unconcerned because my mother had very nicely told me to mind my own business, but that was very difficult since my sister's pregnancy was always in my heart, following me everywhere I went—even right into my dreams. That weekend Mohau was going to be at the wedding and Keitumetse was very excited about that. At that time he had become less and less concerned about being seen and harassed by the police. Seeing her excited and not distressed, it was hard to keep trying to talk about big decisions she had to make. I stopped mentioning it, hoping to make it easier for her, even if I was worried about her so much that I was barely able to calm down.

The wedding brought out the kind of energy that made us believe we were living in happier times. It was a White wedding, which meant that the bride would be wearing a white dress and a veil that was so long that the first bridesmaid would have a lot to hold on to. It also meant that it was the kind of wedding that White people had. The position of the first bridesmaid was very prestigious, and every girl I knew coveted it. The importance of being so close to the bride was not to be underestimated.

Everyone came out in their best clothes. It was a competition without anyone really saying so. We all went to the hair salons to get the perfect perm and look like we just stepped out of a fashion magazine. The bridesmaids had someone do their makeup at a different house on a different street, all of them except for the first bridesmaid, who went wherever the bride would be. My mother got a day off after telling her *missies* that one of her daughters was in trouble. She did not think it was inviting the evil eye since, technically, one of her daughters *was* in trouble. Mama, Keitumetse, and I stepped out in clothes we had just purchased at PEP, the country's most trusted discount store.

I wore a shiny, long blue dress while my sister had something similar on, only shorter and of a different colour. My mother wore clothes that I imagined she would wear if she were the kind of person who cared to dress up and look pretty for church. Her hair was neatly platted, her shoes were very shiny (she had worked on them with some polish and an old piece of pantyhose), and she also wore a hat to go with her dress. Her dress was stunning, it accentuated her figure. She was in powder blue and white. You would have thought we were close personal friends of the bride, but that was just how much effort everyone put into weddings. The three of us looked ready to have the time of our lives.

And we were. We had been building our lives around this event for some time, even choosing to put our worries out of our minds for a while. Keitumetse kept saying that the bride—whoever she was—was going to have some serious competition in us. I had forgotten what a poser she could be when she had the chance.

"Every person in that room will turn their heads as soon as we walk in," Keitumetse said. Mama would not respond to this kind of comment and we would never expect her to. She could look good and never say a word about it. It made her seem really graceful, somehow, this ability to put something on for a big event and never make a fuss—never ask either one of us how she looked. But although Mama may have been silent about what she thought of her own looks and never encouraged vanity, Keitumetse and I had gone out and picked it up somewhere the way children pick things up on the street. Not only were we very comfortable with it, but we also rather enjoyed it.

The bride changed four times: after the white dress she wore traditional clothing, then it was fancy clothes where for the first time the wedding entourage did not wear the same clothes as each other, and then, finally, casual. You knew it was a big and prestigious occassion if the wedding party changed more than twice. Every time they changed into something different, they would come out and go up and down the street dancing with the guests. Everyone's mother wanted to be the one to lead and choose the songs. They all wanted a chance to yell "Sixteen!" which is a request for a change of song. We would dance and sing for about half an hour while they were in one set of clothing, then while they were gone to change we would just sing on our own at the gate until they came back and we started going up and down the street again. There is a reason dancing is known as *thuntsha lerole*, or shooting the dust. When you are really feeling the music all the way down your legs, it goes and settles in your feet and becomes so heavy that you have to hit your foot really hard on the ground, swaying your body back and forth and from side to side. By the time you are done going up and down the street, your clothes look like you have just been frolicking in a tub full of dust. We took our celebrations very seriously.

While some may have been sceptical, the White guests had indeed made their way to the township. Mma Pitse had prepared a table inside the house for them. It was as well prepared as the one the bride and groom would be sitting at. The white cloth and fancy glasses were there, even the fork and knife, a sure sign of upper-class entertainment. They were not sitting in the tent like everyone else—they were special guests. We kept walking past the windows just so we could get a good look at them. We were certain that they had not been in the country very long—someone said they were German and someone else said they were American. Either way, I thought, it explained why they felt they could come and sit here among us. They were obviously not from this country. And they almost looked comfortable, a sure sign they did not have a good idea about who we were, at least not the way White South Africans thought they did. I could tell they saw themselves getting up and walking out of there looking and feeling just fine; they didn't have the same look of terror you saw in White people in town. You could not feel too sorry for these people. They did not look like all they wanted to do was get past you and everything in their world would be okay. They did not look afraid of us or as if they wished they had not laid their eyes on us.

Instead, they seemed almost confident, which made me laugh. I said to my sister, "They almost look like they live here." We joked about going over to them and speaking Setswana, just to see what would happen, but we were not that bold.

Keitumetse said, "I would not be surprised if some comrades came here and actually asked them to help clean up," and I felt a little sorry for them, thinking of how the comrades could actually come and tell them to sit with everyone else under the tent. It was possible they would be told to not act better than everyone else. I half wished they would leave before it got dark. These were not peaceful times.

Just then I remembered Mohau.

"Was he not supposed to be here?" I asked Keitumetse..

"I don't know," my sister said anxiously. "It's late now and Mama will probably want us to go home soon because she has to wake up early for work."

"Maybe we should ask his grandfather," I suggested, but she did not want to face him. She felt uncomfortable speaking with him, because she was thinking about how she would have to speak to him about her pregnancy soon, and she was not ready for it. She and my mother had not formally performed the custom of letting Mohau's family know that she was having a baby. We were also unsure about whether Mohau had told his family, but we both knew that his grandfather had probably already heard the news through the grapevine.

We sat and drank the ginger beer that Mama had helped make the week before the wedding and ate the cookies overflowing from buckets in the kitchen. People always made enough for everyone to take home. But Mohau never came to the wedding. I resented him because my sister was obviously quite disappointed. By the time we left, we had already asked Mama to wait a little longer so many times that she had lost her patience, so we had to go without seeing him.

❊

At two o'clock in the morning, Tshepo and Mohau's grandmother came banging on our door, begging us to wake up and let her in.

"I heard from some boys that the police took them. All of them." I noticed that her eyes were moist once she came in and sat down.

"Who? Who?" Mama kept trying to understand.

"My boys, and everyone . . . Everyone . . . There . . ." She was sobbing and trying to speak at the same time.

Keitumetse turned her back on all three of us as if we had just taken something precious from her. Without saying a word, she went to our room and cried alone as if we had no way of understanding what she had just heard. I felt alternately cold and hot, and I was unable to stand any longer. Mohau's koko, or grandmother, was sitting on a chair in our kitchen with her head in her arms.

"The police say they found them burning tires on the main road, blocking traffic," she told us.

"But when? Today? When we were at the wedding? Today?" Mama kept repeating her question, as if by doing so the whole thing might begin to make sense.

"Yes, today . . . Today . . . my girls too . . . everyone."

This is it, I thought. It was what I had been waiting for since that day in the park when Tshepo first asked me if I could make a petrol bomb. This is it, I kept saying over and over in my mind. My head was throbbing and I was a little dizzy. I could not decide. Koko had come to ask us to use the phone so that she could contact her sister, who lived in another township half an hour away, and ask if she could come and drive her to the prison.

"I don't even know where they took them," she said to me and my mother. "Their grandfather is so worried that I think he is sick, his blood pressure is starting again. *Iyoo, bana.* Children!" She was beginning to speak only to my mother at this point, and I felt like she was asking me to leave the room without saying so. Just then Mama asked me to get on the phone, call Thato's mother, and tell her we needed her to drive us somewhere.

I hesitated only a moment, but quickly reminded myself that this was bigger than whatever was going on or not going on with Thato and me. I was surprised at how quickly I dialled the number; I didn't even have to look it up. I resented that about myself, that I still thought of her so much and remembered everything about her so well, when she seemed to have completely forgotten her friendship with me.

"Hello?" Thato's mother said in a husky, sleepy voice.

"Mama Thato?"

"Tihelo? *Ke eng?*" I knew the sound of my voice had shot the sleep right out of her because she sounded so concerned.

"Mama—" I began.

Koko took the phone from my ear, saying, "Mma Moroka, they've taken my boys . . . to prison . . .thank you."

Within minutes both of Thato's parents were at our house and a mini conference had begun that I was not allowed to be a part of. I got busy trying to comfort Keitumetse, who was more distraught than all the people in the kitchen put together. She just would not stop sobbing. I felt really helpless sitting on her bed, all out of things to say. My fears ran around in my stomach, my head, and up and down my back with no one to calm them but myself. I must have seemed less upset than anyone else because no one seemed concerned about me getting through the night. My mother came in and told us they were all leaving for the police station, and then said to me, "Help your sister calm down, Tihelo, we are just going to find out what is going on." I obeyed Mama's request, rubbing my palm against Keitumetse's chest to comfort her.

Morning found us with eyes wide open. We had been waiting anxiously for the parents to come back from the police station, dreading the news. When Mama finally walked in at six o'clock, I could not decide if she looked more upset or simply very tired. She walked into our room and sat on my bed, where I was sitting and trying to wrap my arms around the entire lower half of my body for comfort. Keitumetse looked up with so much hope I could not bear to see her face. Mama must have felt the same way because she looked at her really hard as if to warn her to step away from that hope. She rested her head on her shoulder, took a deep breath and started to talk:

"I don't know much more than I did when I left here earlier," she told us quietly. "I wish I had better news ... Keitumetse, you have to pull yourself together, this kind of thing has happened before. You know he has been detained and he came back last time. You will have to react better than you did a few hours ago. That is just not going to help anyone. We are all really concerned about those children." She paused a minute and then clicked her tongue, adding, "Koko ... it's so sad."

"What did the police say?" Keitumetse asked, finally speaking for the first time.

"Nothing. They just made us wait for hours and then they told us none of the prisoners were going to get out of that place for a long time."

"Koko has most of her family in prison," I said, thinking out loud.

"The two of them have very brave children, it's just hard to see it that way when your children get punished for their bravery," Mama said. "Keitumetse, what was going on? Why were they burning tires on the road? Were they going to necklace someone?"

Some comrades had been known to get violent and put a tire around someone's neck, setting it on fire. But the SASO people had never done that to anyone in the time that I had known them, so this was a shocking thought for me.

"I thought he was coming to the wedding, I really didn't know about the road or tires or any of that."

"I wonder what they were doing. I hope we find out," Mama said.

Keitumetse panicked, "What do you mean? You think we'll never see them again? What do you mean, Mama?"

"*Ha-e*, Keitumetse, I just mean I hope they don't keep us waiting for nothing next time. I hope they actually let us see them. Their grandparents might sleep better if they let them see their children and grandchildren." She clicked her tongue again. "It's not right. *Iyoo!* National Party, they've taken away our lives."

Mama told her boss at the cafe that there had been an emergency in the township and she would have to come in late. She washed, got in a taxi, and went to work that morning just as she would have any other day. I wanted things to feel somewhat normal, and even though I thought it was unfair that she could not miss work that day, I also thought her leaving for town as usual brought a feeling of continuity, which I needed after the long night.

It was Monday and the beginning of the last week for the Black schools before winter holidays. I heard that the White schools, including the one Thato went to, had two more weeks to go before their break. People were so enraged over the arrests that it was rare to see anyone from the township who went to those schools actually getting past the roadblocks that were beginning to stop all traffic headed towards town. When I arrived at school, there was hardly anyone there. Lebo was packing whatever belongings she had in her desk, saying that she had heard the school would be petrol-bombed any day now. The arrests had only managed to fuel people's fury. We were fully at war, whether or not the police liked it. People were past pretending they had schools to go to. It was about to get much worse.

I kept thinking about the SASO headquarters, wondering if most of those people arrested were people who went there. I thought it would be dangerous to actually go there, but part of me also doubted that the police would have found it. I wanted to go there and see what was happening, but mostly to see if there was anyone left and if they knew what had happened that Sunday. I was just afraid of finding the police.

At home Keitumetse was moping around, not eating or drinking very much. Her worry consumed her and I honestly could not blame her, I felt it too. The hardest part was walking past Mohau's house and greeting his grandfather, who would be sitting under the tree quietly staring into space. I wanted to say something, but I had nothing comforting to say because I was not feeling much better than he was. I really wanted everyone back, especially Tshepo. I assumed he would probably be the youngest one of that group since he was really the most involved person my age that I knew. Most of the others were older, either in their last or second last year of high school. They were mostly sixteen and over. I worried and wondered what would happen to him in prison, if they would treat him any better than they had treated the older ones. Surely they would see that he was only fourteen, I thought. But I honestly could not be sure. The dogs did not operate on reason.

Keitumetse was having second thoughts about being pregnant. She thought maybe she was making a mistake, she did not want a child she would be forced to raise on her own. If she was going to have this baby, she told me, it would have to be with Mohau.

"I don't know if I want to be eight months pregnant and still wondering where he is," she told me.

"I think maybe we should ask someone who might know what to do. Someone who is not likely to tell Mama, but I can't think who that may be," I said.

"Maybe Ausi Martha? She knows her herbs."

"No," I cautioned. "She could never resist telling Mama. Plus, I wouldn't want her revelling in your misfortune. She always finds that so easy."

"Who do you suggest then?"

"I can ask Lebo again. I don't think she would tell anyone. First of all, she doesn't trust parents, and second of all, she likes me enough to keep it to herself. She would never want me to think she is not to be trusted."

"So what will you tell her?" she asked anxiously.

"I won't tell her it's you. I already told her it was a cousin of ours."

"Okay," she agreed quietly, cautiously.

I would take care of it. It would be over soon.

Keitumetse's birthday comes with the spring. Trees in our backyard begin to blossom, little balls of green unripe fruit are being born. The dust of August has settled, and it is no longer difficult to hang wet clothes on the clothesline. More rains will come with lightning and thunder, but right now they are just quick afternoon showers. If we are playing on the street and the rain comes, we go inside and watch it pour and then return to the damp ground an hour later. There are names for different kinds of rains. The slow, drizzling one is medupe. *It is the kind that goes on all day, takes its time to leave. The loud, stormy quick one, the kind that drills potholes in the ground and leaves long convoluted grooves that do not allow cars to enter is called* matlakadibe *(bearer of evil). We have just had the first rain of spring,* kgogolammogo *(one who cleans up the dust).*

My sister wakes up in the morning anticipating the best day she will have all year. We are excited, waiting for Mama to come in and wake us up. She is always telling her boss she is sick and almost never works on our birthdays. I climb off my bed and run to the door. Keitumetse is pretending to be asleep. I am going to find Mama so that we can sing and open my sister's presents. But she is not in her bedroom, so I think she may be in the kitchen, but she is not there either.

I hear voices outside. Mama is speaking to someone, a man. I walk closer to the door and I hear her voice sounding distressed, and the man is sniffing like he is crying. They are talking really softly so I have to come closer to hear what they are saying. I step out softly, quietly on my bare feet. But my mother somehow feels my presence, so she turns around and opens her arms, inviting me to come to her. I go and sit on her lap, but I do not recognize this man who is sitting next to my mother, wiping tears from his cheeks. I put my hand on my mother's cheek and kiss her mouth, something that always makes her smile, but I only manage to get a dull, forced stretch of her lips. "Ke eng, Mama?" I ask her. "What is it?"

"Nothing," she responds feebly. "Go inside and I will come and give Keitumetse her presents." Keitumetse has got impatient, so she is standing at the door. My mother says something to the man and he leaves quietly. After he leaves we sit at the kitchen table and give Keitumetse her presents. There is no feeling of celebration, but my mother is trying. After Keitumetse sees them all and says thank you, my mother tells us: "Steve Biko is dead." We know this is bad, really bad, because recently people have been talking about him constantly, wanting him released from police custody. Students have been rioting, boycotting everything. As the day goes on people are coming in and knocking on our door, speaking to my mother about what has happened. The township mourns. But on the radio, the music keeps playing, the reporter speaks of the weather and sports. Life goes on as normal.

10

AT HER HOME, Lebo and I sat at her kitchen table talking about everything but her father. I did not ask if he was home, I thought that she would not have invited me in if he was. She was loud and relaxed like she always was at school. She poured me a cup of tea and sat back in her chair, and began to address my reason for being there.

"My friend said only half of this should be enough," she said, pointing to a little Coca-Cola bottle that was on the table, filled with a green liquid.

"What is in it?"

"Medicine," she said casually. "It works, trust me. This is someone who has used it before, I know."

"What kind of medicine?" I asked anxiously

"Things that she mixes together, I don't know what she puts in it, but it works."

I felt unsure, but since Lebo said this woman was someone who knew her herbs well, I thought I would not ask too many questions and tried to be more optimistic and trusting. The only problem was that I was worried Keitumetse would not feel as hopeful. She would probably be too afraid.

"Tihelo, this works," Lebo said, trying harder to convince me. "This woman has had so many abortions, and she is still fine. She really trusts this."

"And you trust her?"

"I do. She knows what she's doing. I think it is better than a wire! Believe me, you don't want to give your cousin that option."

That was all I needed to hear. I decided that the green liquid without a name was probably our best option, and it would be subtle. Mama would probably believe us when we said it was just a miscarriage because there would not be any sign of foul play. Everything would be over in a little while, and Mohau would never know. I thought of nothing else all the way home, putting all my faith in the world in that little Coca-Cola bottle. And I hoped that my sister would feel rescued.

Keitumetse was relieved when I gave her the liquid. "I think I'll take it now before I go to bed," she said to me, sitting at the kitchen table and staring at the medicine with as much scepticism as I had done when I was at Lebo's house.

"Lebo said it works really well. This woman she got it from has had a lot of abortions, she used it every time and she really trusts it." I was trying to convince both of us. Keitumetse went ahead and took one long sip of the green liquid. Half an hour after she drank it Keitumetse was sitting on the toilet, bleeding heavily.

"I think this is the way it's supposed to be," she called out to me. I sat on the floor leaning against the wall, exhausted with fear.

"How much longer do you think?" I was asking a question I knew neither one of us knew the answer to.

She would try to get off the toilet, take the biggest pad we had in the house. We would try to go to sleep, but less than an hour later she would be back on the toilet. I thought of calling someone, Thato's mother maybe, to take us to the hospital. My sister's eyes looked worn. She was losing colour and could hardly stand. I thought that I should go for help, but I could not leave her there in the house alone as she was looking worse and worse. Mama came in a little while later, asking why the whole house was dark.

"Why are all the lights off? What are you doing?" We both lay on Keitumetse's bed as I was trying to cool her hot face with a cold cloth.

By the time Thato's mother came over I thought my sister was no longer alive. I wished I could cry. I tried really hard to stop my hands from shaking and to push my feet to move faster. Mama was yelling at me to close the windows, turn on the lights, lock the door, and bring some things for Keitumetse, who was barely conscious at that point. In the car her limp head lay on my mother's lap, her eyes dull and her face pale. My head kept spinning and I was wringing my hands to keep them from shaking.

Thato's mother did not even ask me what had happened—she was a nurse, she would obviously had known—and when I thought about that I realized my mother had not asked either, and I truly believed my whole life was flashing right before my eyes. It was my longest ride to the hospital. True, the nearest hospital was almost an hour away and that was long in any emergency, but it felt like forever. I kept looking out the window at the men and women walking home from work in the dark, but they could not capture my attention. My sister's body was limp and her eyes stared dully into space, her lips turning purplish. I wondered what my mother was thinking. Did she think I was responsible? Did she know I was responsible? Trying to think of whether or not she would eventually give me a long talking to was my way of thinking beyond that car ride. It was my way of visualiszing us back at home, having survived all of this and realising how close we had come to losing my sister.

As soon as we burst into the emergency room the doctors came and took my sister away. None of us were allowed to go in with her. Mama Thato went to speak with the other nurses she knew, and my mother and I were left sitting side by side on a narrow bench in the waiting area. Finally she said to me, "Where did you get it from? Martha?"

"No," I answered, and pretended there was nothing more to say.

"What was it?"

"Medicine . . . green liquid in a bottle." I thought she was going to slap me.

"We have to tell the doctors that, and you may have to tell them where you found it and who gave it to you." She said "you" in the plural form. I hoped she still had no clue which one of us had got it.

"Tihelo," Mama Thato called to me from the reception where she was speaking with another nurse. I looked to my mother for help, but she gave me this look that said, Go ahead, don't look at me.

I felt all the nurses staring at me, wondering what kind of a sister I was. I had made up my mind that they all really hated me.

"What did she take?" Mama Thato asked. "We have to tell the doctor."

"I don't know."

"You don't know?" She made my response sound ridiculous.

"It was just some kind of medicine. A green liquid."

"What was it supposed to do?" she asked. "Who gave it to you? Another doctor?"

I desperately wanted the earth to open up and swallow me. I may have been standing for no more than a minute, but it felt like my whole life. All the nurses' eyes were on me, waiting.

"I got it from a friend of mine. It was supposed to make her get her period."

One nurse who stood behind me gasped and another one put her hand on her mouth and stared at me in horror. I looked back to see what my mother was doing, and she was just sitting upright with her hands on her lap, looking at a child playing in front of her. I was somewhere between her and the nurses when one of the doctors who had taken Keitumetse in came out and called my mother, who got up and followed him inside. I just stood there watching her go, unable to feel my legs.

I was alone a long time sitting on that bench, going in and out of sleep. I had no idea what was going on with my sister or my mother because neither one of them had come out. People were sitting with their families waiting for someone to come and tell them what had happened to their sisters, fathers, mothers, or brothers. None of us looked too hopeful. A tall, skinny man kept getting to his feet and walking up and down the room to calm himself. A woman came in with bruises on her face, her husband sitting quietly next to her. I wondered where she had got the bruises from. They looked familiar, like the kind some women in my neighbourhood had. The ones who had husbands with bad tempers. I could tell how she had got them, I just couldn't tell if it was that very man sitting next to her who had given them to her. I found him sickening, without knowing much about him. It was easy for me to decide his hands were his weapons, I just couldn't understand why he had seen it necessary to bring them in there with her.

The skinny pacing man came over and sat next to me and asked me if I was waiting for my mother. I said that I was and he asked where my father was, to which I answered irritably: "Not here." I must have looked too young to be sitting alone, but I didn't feel young, I felt like I had committed a very adult crime. I wanted to tell him about it so that he would stop being so concerned, thinking I had no business sitting there all by myself. The hospital waiting room was just as terrifying as the police station, especially if you were waiting to hear if someone was alive or not.

"This is like waiting in the police station," I told him, hinting that I had been there and survived it just fine. He looked even more concerned.

"What were you doing in the police station, you're just a little girl," he said, wrinkling his forehead really tight.

"I was waiting for my mother." He shook his head and went back to his pacing.

The child who had been playing in front of my mother was now lying on her mother's lap, sleeping peacefully. The crowd in the waiting room had thinned out, but there were still people coming in on ambulances unaccompanied by family. One man came in with blood flowing down his face. I couldn't look. A woman was running behind him carrying what must have been his shirt because he was topless. She looked just about ready to kill someone. It was as if her fury was pushing him forward, like he had not stopped moving because she was coming for him. They had walked from a nearby township to the hospital, the woman told the nurses at the reception area.

I was both intrigued by and repulsed by them. I wanted to hear her story but I could not look at all that blood. Just as the doctors took them in, my mother came out from behind the large doors, looking really exhausted.

"You can come in and see her," she said, without emotion. I realized just then that it was dawn and that we had been there all night.

As I walked in I turned to see if the skinny man had seen me. He was standing, staring at my mom as if reproaching her for leaving me alone in adult places like hospital emergency rooms and police stations. He had no clue.

We walked silently down a long and dark corridor, passing patients on hospital stretcher beds waiting to be taken care of. I did not want to look at them for fear of seeing something my eyes could not take. But the floors were stained with blood, so there really were not very many places I could look. My mother held my hand all the way down the corridor and I felt temporarily forgiven. We walked for an excruciatingly long time, passing sick people and rushing nurses and doctors who looked like it was all in a day's work. None of them blinked at the sight of their patients. You had to be in awe of how desensitized they were.

We finally got to the ward my sister had been taken to, where were about twenty-four beds, and she was right at the end near the windows. We walked past people who may have looked familiar if I had been able to look their way, but I didn't. I let go of my mother's hand and practically fled to my sister's bed. She was lying there, conscious, with a tube going into her wrist. Her eyes focused on me and her face looked closer to normal than it had in the car, but she seemed really depressed. My mother left me there with her and walked over to speak to someone she knew a few beds over from Keitumetse's. I tried grinning but my mouth just would not stretch that way.

"Don't tell Mama where we got the medicine from," she whispered to me weakly.

All I could manage was a feeble nod. She looked at me and smiled slightly.

"I almost killed you." I said this softly because I did not want Mama to overhear. Being weighed down by that heavy feeling inside my chest, I sat down on a cold narrow bench near the bed and put my head on the bed. I stared at the ground for the longest time, disgusted by the filthy tiles and cockroaches running around on the floor. My sister put the hand with the tube on my head and stroked my hair. I could feel the tube on my neck brushing slightly against my skin, and it made me flinch, but my sister's hand stayed on my head, caressing my hair. Neither of us said another word for the remainder of my brief visit. I hated myself and I hated her for not being careful. I hated my mother for not telling us how to avoid getting pregnant, and I hated Mohau for not keeping his hands to himself. I hated Tshepo for learning about petrol bombs and I hated Thato for escaping. I was incredibly worn out.

Back at home I sat on the bed next to my mother, both of us looking out the window, welcoming the cold winter air coming in. We had hardly said a word to each other the entire way back from the hospital, and I was honestly afraid of what she would say when she finally spoke. The curtains billowed, taking command from the wind. They were yellow and black and many other different colours, but those two stood out most. We had bought them from a woman who came by every week, come hell or high water. She would come into our homes and pull her multicoloured creations out of the large black bag that she carried with her all day. She would not speak until you asked her questions because she was from another country, another part of Africa, and could communicate with us only in broken English. I would stand there and she would show me her curtains and tablecloths, all of which she had sewn herself, and I would be both fascinated and a little baffled by how she looked like she could be from the same street as myself but did not understand a word of what I spoke. I would want to speak with her, ask her how it was over there in that other place, if they lived the same way we did, how she came to choose to be in a place so many of us wanted to leave. She would just go through her work, completely unaware of what I was thinking and not really paying much attention to me. All the while I would be pretending to be interested in something I knew we had no money to buy. In all the years that she had been coming, these curtains were the only things we had ever bought from her.

"We need to wash the curtains. We should have done it in autumn." Mama spoke softly, like she was thinking out loud. "I've missed so many work days lately," she continued, and clicked her tongue.

"Sorry, Mama," I said, putting my head on her lap for the first time since I was about seven or eight years old. She let me, and put a gentle hand on my hair.

"Keitumetse is very strong. She will be home really soon," my mother said. I still had no idea if she knew who had given us the green liquid and I got the feeling it was probably the last thing on her mind.

Here I was with my mother on the verge of losing a job she had worked hard at for so long. Here I was lying on her lap while my sister lay alone in the hospital after miraculously escaping both death and what would have amounted to a life sentence to the township. My friends may be in jail or some other place we did not know about. My neighbours were sitting at home without a single one of their children and neither one of them had the slightest power to go over to the police station and demand answers. People were lying in the hospital to be cured, only to be surrounded by cockroaches. I was faced with the possibility of having to repeat my first year of high school because of the number of classes we had missed. My chances of being ble to study journalism were becoming slimmer everyday.

Here I was living my worst fears and I was still afraid. Afraid of the silence, petrified of men in uniform, and every single night of my life I lay in my bed watching the clock, hoping my mother would make it home. I had not realized that there already had been a night when she did not come home, men in uniform were harassing us every day, and people I knew had already been to jail and back. I was living in the township where all the things I feared were the order of the day. It occurred to me that if I did not make it to university, I would have done nothing in the meantime to improve my chances, instead I would have lived there every day being scared, waiting for something to go wrong when everything had already gone wrong. I was waiting for a stay-away, a riot, tear gas, but they had come and gone many times in my lifetime. It was now the second time that I had almost lost someone in my family. I may have already lost Tshepo and Mohau. What was there to be afraid of? What was left for me to see?

For the first time since I was a child, I was crying. My body was shaking and my mother was so startled, she stopped stroking my hair rather abruptly for a minute before she resumed.

"*Lela*, Tihelo, go ahead and cry, you never cry. Children need to cry . . . go on," she said. It took me forever, shedding that heavy feeling little by little, my chest heaving as I sobbed, mourning our childhood—mine, my sister's, Tshepo's, and Mohau's.

My earliest memory is of feet in black shoes and black socks running, bodies in black and white diving, school bags dropping on the ground in the middle of the streets. Gates are opening and shutting, people are knocking on the neighbour's door, people are banging on our door. Loud, deafening noise resonating all around the neighbourhood. I am standing at the window watching. The people in black and white are throwing stones and dustbins at someone in a large vehicle that is almost higher than the houses. My mother grabs me and we have to lie on the floor, far from the window.

I ask her why the people are running, and she says, "They don't want to learn in Afrikaans. They want to learn in their own language."

"So why do they have to run?" I ask

"Because the police are shooting at them," Mama says. "They are shooting at schoolchildren."

My mother crawls to the back door and rises to let some people in. Strange people are lying on the floor with us, waiting for the bullets to stop flying. I do not know what they are feeling, but some day I will, some day I will run to dodge bullets, bang on strange people's doors, and beg for shelter.

11

DURING THE NEXT few days the sun shone brightly. It was warmer than was typical for winter, and the air smelled of chimney smoke. Some neighbours burned fires in their coal stoves early in the morning to shield themselves from the cold, even if it was not that unbearable outside. Some had not paid the electricity bill and had to use coal to cook. Mapitse was one of those—she had spent so much money on the wedding that her house was dark for the next month. The streets were deserted because a state of emergency had been declared. Up and down the street hippos—the armoured vehicles earned their name because of their enormity— moved at a snail's pace. There were people in them but you could only see their green helmets and the barrels of large guns sticking out the windows.

I decided to go and see if anyone was at the headquarters. We still had no idea where Tshepo, Mohau, and their aunts were. Their grandfather was not even sitting outside anymore because his health was failing him. Every day he and his wife went to the police station to find their children, and every day they were turned away with a different story. Neighbours rallied around them, comrades came in to see that they were eating and sleeping well. Some people—I did not recognize them—were coming in and running little errands for them, going to the shops and buying them bread, getting them milk. Sometimes someone even came to help clean their house.

I also helped when I was not at Keitumetse's side in the hospital, reading to her, bringing her food, and letting her know what was happening in the outside world. I thought she had decided to brace herself for disappointment because she had stopped asking about

Mohau. She must have been too afraid to find out what was going on. I never said anything either, and since she knew I would not have withheld information from her, it seemed to me that she might have assumed that I knew just as much as she did. But I intended to see what was happening, maybe get a clue as to where the comrades may have been taken. If they were not in Pretoria then they were probably being held in Johannesburg, where there were other SASO headquarters. I might be able to phone comrades there and contact someone who would know where to find them. It made perfect sense that they would have been moved. Not only would it take them away from their closest group of comrades, but it would make it impossible for them to see their families, an even greater punishment.

School had come to an end at some point during that week. Instead of only a handful of students being there, no one was going at all. I had not seen the inside of a classroom since my sister was in hospital, and the only reason Mama did not insist that I go was because she herself knew that I would be the only person wearing black and white in the whole township. The only thing I would get from that would be people calling me a sell-out, *mpimpi*, and I needed that about as much as I needed to have another friend go missing. At that point it felt like everyone I had played with on that street had been detained.

One morning I woke up ready to find some answers. I went to the shop to buy some bread, walking briskly and avoiding the intimidating glares of the men in hippos. Some of them looked at me in that way that makes you aware that you are a woman, that way that makes you feel like your body is exposed. I had heard of what they did to women too, so I had no doubt that their looks were not to be taken lightly. I did not know another way of being more careful except to walk faster and faster. I could not ask a neighbour to accompany me to the shop because I needed to go to the office, and I could not risk just anyone knowing about that.

I went into the shop, bought a loaf of bread and some sweets, then went out and started walking in a different direction. Sometimes I was frustrated and confused because I could not decide if I was being followed by the same hippo or if there were just a lot of them around me. I kept my eyes focused straight ahead of me and let my mind escape, run off to a safer place. It was really hard thinking of the future because it held so much uncertainty. I thought about some things Lebo had told me in school, jokes about some of her boyfriends—she had described to me some really crude things. Things I could not help but laugh at, even though they often made me feel shy. Finally, I got close to the house and from where I stood, about five houses away, it looked really quiet, normal, like nothing unusual was going on.

Just to be cautious, I went around a different street and looked for a house that looked empty so that no one would see me jump over their fence. I remembered how Tshepo and I would climb over people's high fences to get lemons or other fruit in their backyards, and I thought I had had ample training. No matter how high a fence was, it couldn't intimidate me. Slowly and stealthily, I worked my way through people's backyards. I was lucky because none of those people had dogs. I jumped over their fences so swiftly that by the time I reached the backyard of the offices I did not have a scratch to show for it. My bread, on the other hand, looked less than appetizing. I had it tucked under my armpit that whole time and it had been pressed into an hourglass shape.

I looked carefully around me, afraid the hippos towering above the houses would have an easy time seeing me. They were never too far, and I did not want to take a chance at being found. Finally I got to the door, and as I was about to knock I realized that I had forgotten to call and say that I was coming. That meant that whoever was there would not open. Maybe they had seen me long before I arrived, but I had quit so long ago that I could easily be thought of as a spy. Allies kept in touch and stayed supportive, but I had done neither in the previous few weeks.

I decided to knock anyway, I had come so far. But no one answered. There was hardly any sound coming from the inside. I put the bread down and, using the bricks on the ground below the bath-room window, tried to climb in. I succeeded and fell on the bare floor in less time than I had expected. No one came to see what was going on, so I assumed that no one was there. I got on my hands and knees and moved around like a prowler. The house looked surpris-ingly neat and there was no trace of a police raid. My heart settled a little at the sight of everything looking like it was still in place, but I was disappointed not to find anyone. In the room that Tshepo and I had worked in, some of his drawings were on the floor, and there was a huge banner that I thought someone may have still been work-ing on at the time of the arrest because a lot of dust had collected around it. Some old informational fliers that I had helped make were on a table in the same room. They had really old information on them, but I liked looking at my own writing and marvelling at how brave I now thought it was to have come here all those months.

I realized then that if any of the comrades had escaped, they would be here at the office. It was either that or only one or two were left and they weren't here because they had gone underground. They would not want to lead the police to the office. I was hoping that no one had known about me ever coming there—I knew that being four-teen was not going to be enough for the police to not take notice, so I had to be very careful. I felt I needed to get in touch with comrades from Soweto and let them know we had an empty house here, so I went into the front room where the sofa was and sat there trying to think of where the important phone numbers were. They were never kept near a phone because that would have been too dangerous—it would only take one raid to incriminate hundreds of fellow com-rades across the country. I used my elbows to balance my body and climbed onto the sofa like a crawling baby would: arms and hands first and then one leg at a time. I was not about to take a chance and stand up, I thought the men in hippos could probably see through windows even if they were five kilometres away. If I was paranoid it was probably better for my survival. Like they say in Setswana, *Ga bo lefyega a go lliwe.* The home of the paranoid never sheds a tear.

I lay there trying to think of a safe place where the numbers could be hidden when I heard a sudden thump, similar to the noise I must have made when I jumped down from the bathroom window. It also came from the same room. My first instinct was to hide, but I was in a room that was almost completely bare except for the sofa and a telephone. I slipped over to stand against the opposite wall, so that the person coming in would not see me. For a few minutes the person did not move, and I realized that they could not have been the police. First of all, the police had nothing to fear from us when they had their guns. Second, the person had stopped for about the same amount of time as I had before they proceeded.

"*Amandla*?" I whispered. "Power?"

"Awetu . . . Awetu!" the person whispered back. "To the people."

I crawled out of the room and our faces met at the passage like two dogs about to kiss. It was Dikeledi. While I was really relieved to see her there, she looked greatly surprised for a minute. Then she sat back on her heels and allowed herself a sigh, resigning herself to my trust.

"What are you doing here?" she asked.

"Are you the only one left?" I inquired, still on my hands and knees.

"Yes! A lot of the people are underground."

"You mean they're not in detention?"

"Well, some of them are. Mohau's aunts are in detention. He and Tshepo are underground. It's him they're really looking for. They won't release his aunts until they say where he is."

I was relieved to hear that not everyone was in prison. All kinds of thoughts rushed through my head. Maybe I could see his aunts now and talk to Tshepo. I missed him so much, I was so afraid for him. Maybe I could tell his grandparents that they were not in detention, it may make them feel some amount of relief and hope. But it was as if Dikeledi had been hearing my mind race.

"Don't tell the grandparents, okay? We don't want to give them any hope. Mohau and Tshepo are not even in South Africa anymore," she told me very sternly.

"Does he know about my sister?" I asked, suddenly feeling a rush of sadness.

"He does. He's already sent her a message."

That explained why Keitumetse had not asked me any questions. I thought I knew so much more than I did. Why didn't anyone tell me these things? Keitumetse probably felt that the less I knew, the better it would be. People were afraid that if the police asked me questions I would be so intimidated and terrified that I might give away important information. They may have been right, I thought, it must have been obvious to everyone. I had been wearing all the fear in the world on my face for months now. Leaving the headquarters must have alarmed them—they were probably afraid from the time I stepped out.

"Tihelo, I really have to ask you to be extremely careful. Don't come here every day, or even every other day. Once a week, maybe," Dikeledi said, still being very firm.

I said, "I wanted to tell the comrades in Soweto what was going on, that's why I came." I think she almost got us both caught with her little laugh.

"Shhhhh," I cautioned irritably. But I had to admit she was really beautiful when she smiled. I had never seen her face glow like that. Her smile drew about two or three lines on either side of her mouth and her eyes sparkled. She looked completely different from the person I knew, who had been so serious and spoken with so much authority. Before this I had never looked at her face for more than just a second. For some time I had found it irritating that she was so strict and serious, and always too busy to chat. That was a big moment for me, I could have watched her smile forever.

"Sorry," she said, putting her hand on her chest as if to stop herself. "You're very helpful, thank you. But the comrades in Soweto know what is going on. They always do. Besides, they are the ones who helped us take our people to the other side. So it's okay, you didn't have to do that."

I felt suddenly small and silly on my hands and knees. "I just wanted to help. I didn't think there was anyone left."

"Thank you. I'm happy I'm not the only one here—and you . . . it would be very helpful if you kept your ear to the ground, just in case. I can't do everything on my own." She was comforting me, being gentle. And she must have thought she was not doing a good enough job because she added, "I have to tell you, I am really relieved to have another comrade here, it's been very hard for me."

I remembered the day I quit the SASO, the last time I was here, when she said to me: "You have been a loyal and faithful comrade. You are brave." I was happy she was the one left and that we would be working together. I thought, She may not know it now, but I am not as afraid as I used to be. I will be an even more loyal comrade than I was before. From then on, if anyone was going to be in the kind of trouble my sister had been in, we would have to have access to the right kind of help. My neighbours needed their children back at home and I wanted to be of some help to them. But most of all, I wanted to see myself safely in school the next year. I had places to go and things to do in places I had known for longer than I could remember.

Mma Kleintjie had obviously been her usual watchful self because she had more information than I had bargained for when she saw me walking back to the house that afternoon. She startled me for the first time in ages. The sun was just going down, a time when everyone had to be indoors because of the state of emergency. We had to make sure that none of us were on the streets after the sun set, and our lights had to be out by nine o'clock at night. The government had intended to keep an eye on us, and we had to be contained in places where they could do that to the best of their ability. While the police had the government's permission to violate our rights daily, any disobedience of their commands could lead to detention and a million other things that we would not wish on our worst enemies. All of us, no matter how old, were living like children under the watchful eye of a vengeful adult.

Well aware of the repercussions of being found on the street after dark, I rushed to get home before someone saw it necessary to climb down from a hippo to interrogate and harass me. But when I reached the gate of our house, there she was standing right in front of me. She had this incredibly annoying skill of sneaking up on people without making a noise. I had really lost a lot of patience with her since Ausi Martha had so easily convinced me that the only reason this woman was interested in me was because of my light skin. I hated anyone who made me so aware of my difference in the township. It had become very important to me to stay away from her, but she always managed to find me when I least expected it. The only difference was that I was no longer the fearful child I used to be, I would stand and look her straight in the eye when she approached me.

"I have to go inside, sorry," I said, pushing past her.

"You watch your sister," she told me, and I froze. "You tell her they are coming for her." She turned and started to walk away.

"What do you mean?" I almost yelled, but I realized that doing so would only get me the wrong kind of attention. "Who is coming?"

She turned around and said, "I know everything, you just ask me. Tell your sister they are coming for her." She ran back over to her house and left me standing there with about a hundred questions.

I closed the gate behind me and ran into the house, frantic. I could not phone anyone and tell them. I did not know Dikeledi's number, and Mama would not be home for another two or three hours. It was frustrating sitting there, completely helpless. I thought of going to the hospital but I had no money to leave and get on a taxi. I could have gone to one of the neighbours, but I thought they would tell me to ignore a crazy woman. So all I could do was wait. To keep myself busy, I cleaned an already clean house and started cooking supper for me and my mother. Eventually Mama did come home, but she was already ahead of me.

"The police were questioning Keitumetse today," she told me.

"Why?"

"Because they know she is Mohau's girlfriend. They want her to say where he is."

I could hardly stand. "What did she tell them?"

My mother smiled slightly. "She said that he had run away as soon as he found out she was pregnant. She said, 'He did not want the responsibility, so he left me. I have not seen him since.'" As she said that she let out a really sad laugh.

"How did Mma Kleintjie know, then?"

She looked at me as if to say, "Not again!" and I quickly added that she had just come up to me and warned me about Keitmetse.

"That woman is like a ghost. She knows everything, I don't know how."

"It's just that she seemed so sure of what was going to happen, and it did happen."

Mama was getting irritable. "I don't like her. Anyway, I thought it was brave of your sister."

"It was brave. They believed her?"

"I think so. They left her alone, which is what she needs. She will be home tomorrow," she said with a slight smile. We were both relieved, it had felt like she was gone forever. We knew she was very unhappy staying in the hospital, even if she had been looking calmer than we had expected.

12

I COULD NOT STOP thinking about Mma Kleintjie. My lifelong curiosity about her had resurfaced after our latest meeting. When I got past being afraid of, and annoyed with, her, she was really intriguing. It was awful how she just appeared out of nowhere and pretended you were supposed to know she had been there the entire time. Especially in a state of emergency, no one needed to be frightened like that. Apart from that, I thought there was something that drew me to her, but I could not really put my finger on it. I had a lot on my mind apart from her. There was also Keitumetse's return home and the time I was spending with Dikeledi. I had insisted on doing whatever I could to help and be useful at the office. My need to have Tshepo and Mohau back was only getting stronger. I really missed Tshepo. Dikeledi and I had been busy pouring all our frustrations into more newsletters and transcribing some illegal ANC tapes, and the work made me feel like I was doing something towards getting my friends back home. In spite of all the fear in us, we had to keep informing people, letting them know that the struggle was continuing.

Unlike at the beginning of my work at the office, I felt that I was fully involved in deciding what shape my life would take. It no longer seemed like someone else was dictating it all for me. Although Mama knew where I was going one or two afternoons a week, we never discussed it and I had no idea how she felt about my work at the SASO. Perhaps it was clear to her that I was feeling more in control and less timid. The fear had not disappeared, however, I was just learning to use it to serve me better. It was obvious that if we sat at home waiting for someone to decide that it was time to stop detaining our friends and neighbours, we would have to wait all our lives. So I viewed my work at the headquarters as something that might speed up the process of ending laws that prevented me from going to school. Laws like the Bantu Education Act and other discriminatory acts that denied Tshepo's grandparents the right to be with their children or simply know where they were at any given moment. I was not free of the fear, it had just ceased to be paralyzing.

*

During the transition from middle to high school, I was not as obsessive about my light skin as I had been in previous years. I saw it as secondary to all the other concerns that kept coming up, and both my sister and my mother were relieved to see that change in me. I needed my family more and more, and we were now three adults in the house instead of only two. My closeness with my sister and my mother mattered more to me than the things that seemed to set me apart from both of them. Occasionally I would spend some time before going to bed wondering about my difference, but it was never as consuming as it had been before high school. Life was presenting me with more challenges, ones that were more demanding of my attention, and I had no time to lie down and watch the seasons change or think about the weather's effects on my backyard while basking in the scorching sun. Also, no one at the headquarters ever commented on my skin colour. They were always so serious about work, and I felt I had to shift my focus from myself to work. But it was not completely out of my mind. I still wondered why my hair was so much softer than my sister's and why neither my mother nor my sister bruised as easily as I did or why it was really only the shape of my body that reflected theirs.

One day in school Lebo suggested that I may only be Keitumetse's half-sister, and I found myself unable to disagree. It was one of those moments when someone says something you have been thinking of but had been too afraid to say out loud—it was too distressing to have it put on the table and laid bare for me to fully examine. As much as I wanted to discuss my difference, I had to dismiss Lebo's idea because it was too painful to admit that I may only be half related to my sister.

While Keitumetse was in the hospital, during that time when I thought I might be losing her, I wondered about our differences again. I began to allow myself to think of the possibility of having relatives I had not met before. When I kept thinking, Oh my God! I may have killed the only sibling I've ever had in my life, I could not help but wonder if she really was the only one. It was, of course, a safe diversion for me. I could always go places that felt safer because not only did it make me feel more able to handle what I was faced with in reality, but it also did not hurt anyone. I was not asking anyone questions that made them uncomfortable—at least no one other than myself. It was important for me to notice the great discomfort this subject brought everyone, I had no intention of bringing back those old resentful looks to my mother's face. At this point I needed to have a relationship with her that was as simple as possible. It was my excuse for not going to any trouble to find answers. I just kept thinking that if it was that hard to just think about what the questions might do to my mother's attitude towards me, then maybe it really was not worth pursuing.

I had also watched Mama go through so many difficult things in the previous few months, I did not want to see her upset. It seemed better to not have her think I doubted the answers she had already given me before, which were that I was her child and no one else's, and that I had no reason to ask more questions. The problem was, she had not told me anything apart from letting me know she preferred not to hear any more about it.

Meanwhile, I was ready for my sister to be home. Since she would be released from the hospital in the afternoon and would be taking a taxi home, I thought she might want to have someone to come home with, so I went there to meet her. As much as I hated the hospital, I was patient enough waiting for her to check out and speak to the nurses, which she had to do before she was allowed to leave. Although she was happy to see me, I was sad about her silence. It was obvious that being in the hospital had taken a toll on her. She had very little energy and looked weary, and it took a lot for her to smile and speak. The music in the taxi was really loud and the driver was going very fast, stopping abruptly to let passengers out. The entire time I held my sister's hand, and she seemed unfazed by the possibility of us being in a car accident. Fortunately, we were both in one piece by the time our stop came, and I complained about the man's driving in an effort to make conversation. Keitumetse said about three words between the time that we got in the taxi and the time we arrived home.

I liked having her at home, it felt a lot more familiar and I felt less uneasy. Although I had not fully realized it, it always seemed like something might go wrong with Keitumetse while she was in the hospital. Mama and I said once or twice that it would feel a lot better if she had been right at home with us so we could see how she was recovering, but the doctors kept saying they had to keep her a while longer. Neither one of us actually thought the healing would begin in the hospital, it was too disconcerting a place for a person to truly rest and feel at ease.

Even once she was home, Keitumetse said next to nothing about Mohau. He was a cloud hanging over us. She had not seen him in a long while, and had gone through more than her share of crises in that time, so I expected her to say she missed him. I thought she would also want to talk about her experience in the hospital, but I was wrong. It was obvious to me that my sister was feeling heavy and exhausted, but she stayed calm and pretended to feel nothing. She looked a lot more serene than she had ever seemed in all the time that I had known her. It was strange how that pregnancy seemed to have changed her whole character. She did not seek comfort as easily as she had done before. In fact, she never sought comfort from Mama and I at all. We felt uneasy with this new part of her.

Both my mother and I had prepared ourselves for a woman who would come home and demand all of our attention. We were ready to be the caregivers that we thought she would need us to be, but she never asked for anything from us. I ran around trying to do everything for her, my behaviour bordering on obsessive. I must have asked her if she needed anything about a hundred times a day, my way of overcompensating for what I thought was essentially my fault. But instead of being annoyed, or even grateful, my sister was like a lifeless doll with a fixed smile. She looked polite, as if she had to be there without choice and she was doing the best she could to make it as painless as possible for all of us, including herself.

"Are you feeling angry about the medicine?" I asked one night as I sat by her side on her bed. I was really just begging for reassurance.

"No," she said politely.

"Are you feeling angry with Mohau for not being here?"

"No."

After she said this I took a deep breath and asked the question I did not want answered.

"Do you think I did it on purpose? Do you think I tried to hurt you?"

"Of course not," she said sincerely.

"Oh," I said, frustrated. I paused a while and then something else occurred to me. "Are you sad about the baby?"

"No."

"I heard sometimes women feel guilty. Do you feel guilty? Like you did something wrong?"

"No!" This time she was firm. "I don't feel guilty about the pregnancy, I feel relieved. Tihelo," she said, grabbing my hand, "I'll never regret that. I regret not asking someone more reliable about what to do, and maybe I also regret not telling Mama what I was planning, it was a careless and irresponsible way to do it. But even if you had not got me the medicine, I would still be running around trying to find another way to end the pregnancy."

So she had given me answers and I had no more questions left to ask, but I was still very dissatisfied, although I did not know why. I continued running around trying to speed her recovery by cooking, offering her fruit, and getting her drinks. But my sister remained quiet, removed, and always gentle with me. It was almost as if I would have preferred to be yelled at. I kept thinking it would be better if she were really angry with me, but she was not. She seemed so far away that most days it was impossible to reach her.

13

KEITUMETSE WAS HOME about a month before Tshepo's aunts were released from detention. I had never really been close to either one of them because of the wide age gap between us, so I did not feel as if I could speak with them. They did not return to the office and rarely left their home. Every day they would come out of the house, clean the *stoep* and sweep the yard, and then lie on a blanket on their front lawn, right next to their father's chair. Both of them were so depressed that they said almost nothing to me when I went to their house. All they did was answer my questions with a yes or a no. I had to communicate with them, because as a fellow comrade it was my responsibility to make sure that they were in good health. More people had returned to the office, mostly those who had just come back from detention. All of us had our duties set, we knew what had to be done and divided our work accordingly. I was going to different houses making sure that the comrades were surviving. I brought them news and asked if they needed anything. Most of them needed medical help because of the torture they had been through in detention. Part of my duty was to arrange for them to see a doctor. I had to do many illegal things like learn to drive even though I was underage—I needed to, it was absolutely necessary. We would go into people's houses up on the hill, the richer people, and ask them for their cars for the day. They had no choice but to oblige because as comrades we commanded a lot of respect and were all in all a force to be reckoned with in the townships. These cars we took from people would help us do things like take ex-detainees to the hospital for treatment and for any other kind of therapy they needed. We would also use them to go and buy groceries for families whose main providers were in detention. Eventually the cars would become useful for more duties than we would have liked. They became emergency vehicles, used for driving around the outskirts of the *lekeishene* looking for bodies of missing people. Sometimes we would find people who had been beaten by the police and left for dead in garbage dumps.

At this point I forced myself to return to school because I believed that I needed to. We did not all agree on that point, a lot of people felt that we had to have our demands met before we set foot on government property. Personally, I needed that sense of continuity. I would read schoolbooks that I knew we were supposed to be using. I would enlist a few interested parties in a study group. I hoped that being in school would make me feel like I was maybe going to finish in time—I hoped I would not have to repeat any classes. Basically, I hoped for a miracle. People thought I was a hypocrite, pursuing the education that was forced on me by the very people I was writing and marching against on a weekly basis. But I knew I really had no other way of making myself believe I would get out of there alive. I had to go on believing that I would eventually leave, otherwise I could not fully be a comrade. My efforts at the headquarters would feel pointless. I felt I could not do one or the other, I had to keep both going. Someone even told me that I put on a different mask when I went to school, that I wanted the dogs to see me as someone who was a good, school-loving child. But I really was not doing it for anyone but myself and my family. What would have been hypocritical was if I had risked my sister's life so that she could be guaranteed to leave, and then spent every day of my life burning tires and sending out newsletters, completely forgetting that I had to study in order to be a journalist.

It was not as if I did not understand the confusion. It was infuriating reading some of the things I had to read in class. My history books said the history of South Africa began in 1652, when the Dutch East India Company set foot on the southern tip of the continent. I ground my teeth throughout those study sessions because everything was so badly written, there was so much misinformation, and it was all obviously deliberate. There were sentences about Black people, migrant workers, that would say things such as, "These people could not even feed their own families." Right after it was mentioned that the government went to great lengths to make sure Africans got the most meagre salaries and that workers had to move far away from home to make a living. I was educating myself on someone else's ignorance and that was my only way of getting myself to a better place. At the same time, everything worth reading was banned so most of us had no access to it. The only exception was those of us who were writing newsletters, reading books, and listening to tapes that were banned under many government laws.

Sometimes, after I had finished typing out information pamphlets or essays for the newsletter, I would sit and read about men and women who had risked their lives the same way that we were doing, but who had either been killed by the government or were now in jail. Information about women freedom fighters was hard to come by, yet I knew from my experience that there were many of us, from many different age groups.

It was not hard to understand why the men's efforts were better documented. They had a way of taking over and making it look like it was only them fighting for women and children, when in reality no one person held a role more important than the other. I knew about the women's march on parliament in 1958. I read about women like Albertina Sisulu and Winnie Mandela, who were made to look like they were targeted only because their husbands were so prominent in the ANC, but who in fact were comrades in their own right. I also knew without having to read about it that many women I had grown up around were detained and had been tortured. Even our mothers, who were enduring a lot of abuse from their bosses, continued to work because they had to feed and clothe us. I spent a lot of time reflecting on what I was doing there as an SASO member, and wondering if someday some history book would acknowledge that there were many women working and risking their lives in that house, and elsewhere in South Africa.

After all that time, I still had no idea what exactly had happened that Sunday evening when most of our friends were taken away. There were quite a few who had still not returned from detention. Tshepo and Mohau remained out of the country, and I still had not found out how that had come to be. I could not ask their aunts, but I asked some of the comrades at the house. Thabang, the one who had greeted Tshepo and I on my first day there, had also been arrested. He told me what had happened as we were sitting at the kitchen table stuffing envelopes for mail we were about to send out.

He was shocked to hear that I still thought they had been caught making a roadblock.

"*Wena!* Why hasn't anyone told you yet?" he said.

"I don't know. We've all been working so much, I didn't have a chance to ask."

"We were having a birthday party at my home—it was my twenty-first. None of us were on the streets. The police got a tip from someone that we were there and so they just came in unexpectedly. Mohau and Tshepo were behind the house and they escaped very swiftly." Thabang laughed lazily. "I'm impressed with them, you know? They hid at my next-door neighbour's house for the whole night. Someone got them out the next day."

"*A-o?* Is that so?" It made sense that the police would have had people's families believe that they had been doing something illegal.

"You know why they came for us, right?" Thabang continued.

"No, why? They had been looking for you, huh?"

"No, what was happening that Sunday that was unusual in the township?"

"What?"

"Remember, just think back."

"I don't know, I don't remember anything unusual."

"Didn't you go to a wedding with mama *hao* and Keitumetse?" he asked, with a slight smile on his face.

"*Ja* . . . what? The wedding?"

"Who was at the wedding?" He said this as he continued stuffing envelopes. I felt absolutely clueless for a while and then I stopped.

"The White people?" I asked.

"*Ja!*" he continued.

"What about them? No one went after them, did they? Did they think you . . . oh! Ah!" I exclaimed, my hand on my mouth.

Thabang said, "They wanted to make sure the White people got out of the township safely. Mapitse told the police they were coming and the police wanted them to be safe. So they came after us, locked us up, and I guess you could say they forgot why they had locked us up. We assumed we were only going to be there for a day, but they just kept us. One of them was saying they had evidence that we were going to cause trouble, because we had been known to do it before."

"Serious?"

"Serious."

We carried on with our work.

14

OVER TIME PEOPLE got increasingly anxious about the detained comrades, who did not seem to be coming back home. Families were restless, parents were sick with worry. It was disastrous—we were at a point where we could not be sure that people were still alive. Detention "suicides" were escalating and the police were guaranteed government protection because they were agents of the state, doing the best they could to try and eliminate an entire population. As if there were not enough detainees, there were more and more arrests. Some people were arrested just because they had been standing in a large group and the police were suspicious of their motives. There were stories of people being shot at because the police thought they looked suspicious. Women and men died from flying bullets because they were on the streets after dark, when someone thought they should be in their homes. Friends and neighbours ended up in jail because they just happened to be in the wrong place at the wrong time, and in the township, that was everywhere, all the time. We treaded lightly on our own streets and spoke in hushed tones in our own homes. Nothing felt safe, and we were even suspicious of people we had known and loved for longer than we could remember.

We had to do something. Although we had been talking about it on and off for weeks, there came a time when the SASO had a discreet meeting to discuss the most logical step to take in the next few days. It was clear that the more time we spent talking and doing nothing, the more time people spent in jail.

"We are in a state of emergency," Thabang announced to the group sitting on the floor in the front room of the office. "And I don't mean the kind that the government has declared. We need our comrades and they keep disappearing, going into detention, and we don't even know if some of them really are in there. We don't even know if some of them are still alive. We must do something immediately."

People started speaking to each other around the room, trying to decide what to do.

"The government has declared war on us," Dikeledi added from the back of the room. She always spoke with so much passion that none of us would interrupt when she had the floor. The room went quiet, and I found myself fully attentive, taking in everything from her: her big focused eyes, her perfectly shaped dark lips, her high cheekbones. Her voice was steady, clear, and firm. Everyone in there knew that she felt every word she said. She spoke from deep inside herself.

"Our comrades need us just as much as we need them. We are a family here—whether or not you support the ANC is not an issue. We are all one." Then she added what was probably the most uttered statement in all of Black South Africa: "An injury to one is an injury to all."

Someone sitting on the floor raised their voice—"Viva ANC viva!"—and we all responded: "Viva!"

"Viva Mandela viva!"

"Viva!"

"Viva Sisulu viva!"

"Viva!"

And we all joined in a hushed chorus of *"Senzeni na, Senzeni na e South Afrika?"* What have we done in South Africa?

The meetings and rallies were always moving. We were joined in the spirit of comradeship. We would share food and water, and our mutual respect, and the feeling that we truly had each other to rely on. It was at moments like these that some comrades would announce: "I am prepared to die for my country, I am prepared to die for the truth."

It was hard for me to say that, to allow myself to think that the possibility of my death coming sooner than I'd hoped was very real. In that time it was crucial for me to remind myself that I did not have to be in that house, in that office, breaking the law in order for me to be in grave danger. What I was doing with the ANC had no bearing on whether or not I would be killed or detained by the police. Living in South Africa, being there at that time, was risk enough. I had to remind myself of it and teach myself to never ever think that there was a place where I could be safer. This is what I had been born into and there was no escape—I could either sit at home and be afraid alone, or I could be on the front lines and be afraid with everyone else. Either way, fear was a close companion that had come to stay. It was nothing new; my life had been in jeopardy since long before I was born.

I always had a hard time making that statement because what I really wanted to say was that I was too young to be constantly thinking about my own death. None of us had done anything at all to invite death to come looming in our neighbourhoods. Things had been that way when we arrived. I was involved in the SASO so that I could believe in the possibility of us living in a place where there were no guns aimed at our futures. I reminded myself over and over again of my mother's words: "If you didn't choose to rebel, you would probably be resigning yourself to a life of despair." And that was enough to keep me focused and willing to do whatever I could to bring back our comrades, friends, and neighbours—also, to fight for a different world.

After sharing different ideas for a while we came up with a strategy. We were going to march to the police station and make our demands. We would do this at the nearest station, not in town where most of the comrades were being held. Going into town would have required a lot more organizing; we would have had to take buses and taxis, which would have alerted the police immediately and landed us in jail. The whole operation had to be very well organized, which meant that all of us had roles to play in making sure the police did not find out about the march before it happened. Otherwise we would all be detained before the date of the march. At first I was nervous about having to send out word that we were headed for the police station. We had to make sure we had mass support and at the same time keep the news from reaching the wrong ears. It was obviously difficult and we were taking a big chance, given the presence of spies at every corner—like the people who had told the police about Thabang's birthday party—but we constantly operated on that kind of delicate faith. We had to trust people we did not know, and it was more important to find support than it was to worry about the police sabotaging our plans. This was urgent.

So, on that Friday, in the middle of the rising August dust, days before we could expect the first spring rain, we gathered at Matseke, the high school that some of us, including myself, went to. People had their school uniforms on partly because it was a school day and partly because we wanted to make the statement that it was we, the students, whom the police had upset the most. We knew that most of the people they taken in the previous few months were schoolchildren, and we wanted to let them know that those detainees had our support.

It was going to be a really long march since we had to go all around the township, pass by every school, so that whoever wanted to come along would join us. But we were ready for the journey. Our pleas felt urgent to us and we thought the action we were now taking was long overdue. We had our placards and T-shirts, which were illegal, but we insisted from the beginning that this would be a very peaceful march. We all had such a strong sense of loyalty to one another that none of us had to worry about our agreements being disregarded by any comrade. The police were the only people we had no faith in. But all of us had come to the conclusion that being peaceful and calm would appease the police—they liked being obeyed, and if obedience was what it took to get their attention, then we were willing to give it to them.

Winter being at its tail end, most of us were wearing our black school jerseys, but by the time we had started moving it was so hot that we had to remove them. We sang and danced, as we would have done at any march, because it kept our spirits up and strengthened our will. It also alleviated the dread and made the journey seem short and even better than bearable. We moved up and down the streets hollering our requests, crying out our hopes and wishes. Our acute awareness of the grave danger we live in temporarily subsided, so that all we really felt was power, power, and more power. Moving in great numbers brings this illusion of might. We believed we could accomplish anything we set out to do, even the police could not find this kind of force in their weapons. We may have been young but we were mighty, and we came in large numbers. When we passed by people's houses they could feel our collective power and they sensed the determination within our group. People dropped whatever they were doing to join us. Old women and men sitting in their front yards, basking in the sun, cheered us on. Some were too terrified of the police to support us, so they yelled at their children to get inside the house and stay away from us because we were only looking for trouble.

We were masses moving as one, covered in the dust we were dancing in. From a distance you would probably not have seen people dancing so much as a dust storm rising. Our black shoes and socks wore the powdery, brownish colour of the sand we were swimming in. Our hair looked like we had bathed in the sand and so did our clothes. People who had covered themselves in Vaseline had what almost looked like a mud mask covering their legs, arms, and faces. But all of it was intoxicating, the way power always is.

By the time we reached the police station our journey felt short and quick, although we had just marched for a full hour. Our numbers had also increased quite significantly in all that time. We were hot from the march and we were also standing under the now-scorching sun. The police had been alerted long before we got there, but it was surprising that they had not forced us to disperse sooner. When we arrived at the station, however, they were ready to deal with us. Policemen—both Black and White—stood at the large iron gates, their vans and hippos sprawling all around the building, their guns pointed at us. We felt no panic, we had just come to demand the release of our comrades and then we would be on our way.

Thabang stepped forward in his black "Free Our Leaders" T-shirt, but before he could say anything, one policeman standing high up on his hippo yelled out, "So, you've come to lock yourselves up?" and they all roared with laughter.

Someone among us yelled "Viva ANC viva!" and everyone yelled back "Viva!"

The policemen's guns made a loud click and we shifted among ourselves, but remained quiet so that Thabang could speak. Before he said anything, Dikeledi walked up and joined him and they stood side by side. Thabang started: "We have come to demand the release of our comrades."

A white Afrikaner policeman said, "You know this is illegal and we will lock you up. Do you want to join your friends?"

Thabang continued, "There are presently more than fifty innocent children in your detention centres who were taken from their streets for no reason."

"We will have no criminals here. Go home!" yelled the policeman.

"We will remain here until we see our brothers and sisters walking through those doors. We would like to speak with your chief officer," Dikeledi insisted, her eyes focused on the policeman, who had been yelling back obscenities.

They laughed at us really loudly. "Well, even I don't speak with my chief officer so easily," he responded, much to his co-workers' amusement. I noticed in the distance a policeman holding a long rifle with one arm. His other arm had been cut off so that he only had one full arm, the back of his rifle tucked under his armpit. I thought it was Lebo's father, and it made me dizzy, I thought something was in my eye and that I could not see clearly, so I kept rubbing my eyes, trying to see him better, but I couldn't.

One of them got impatient with something Thabang said and he fired his gun in the air to scare us. But we broke into a song about Oliver Tambo and started dancing to our own music. Another gun was fired in the air and we sang louder and louder. Then the air was hazy and people started screaming and cursing. My eyes stung more and more and my throat felt extremely sore, like someone had just been rubbing it with sandpaper.

People still refused to leave. Instead, boys took off their shirts and girls used their school jerseys as a shield against the gas. But the police were determined to have us leave what they kept calling "police property." One of the men in a large van that was to the left of the crowd started the engine, and that was when we panicked. My first thought was that I wish we had petrol bombs, which was strange because we probably would not have accomplished much with them. The roaring engine of a hippo terrified people and we were infuriated by that terror, because we had been so peaceful and all the police had done was fire their guns and throw tear gas. The hippo started coming towards us and some more engines started up all around the crowd. The police were literally going to drive us off the street.

The force of the hippos coming at us, and the power of the guns and tear gas, brought out an even stronger sense of power in the crowd. We felt disrespected and ignored. We were furious. Still refusing to move, people all around me started to pick up stones from the ground and throw them at the police. I was both horrified and infuriated by the sight of a large vehicle coming towards me, about to flatten our bodies on the ground. Like everyone else, I picked up a stone and threw it at the hippo; I felt like all the power in the world lay in the palm of my hand. That stone—although it was no bigger than the centre of my palm—carried all the force I had within me. It was a moment fuelled by sheer terror, compounded with the passion of the spirit of resistance. I saw in that stone my ticket to freedom. I was about to demolish a war machine along with the man who was driving it towards me.

There was more screaming and cursing. The crowd now scattered, but not as fast as the police had hoped. We reluctantly ran backwards, throwing stones as we attempted to get away. It was all incredibly frustrating—we did not know what we wanted to get away from the fastest, the vans and hippos or the guns. Our will and power of resistance were still there. We probably only moved because the cars were coming at us and not so much because we were afraid. The stones kept flying, hitting large machines that looked like they were made solely of steel, and not really making a difference. A small rock hit the front shield of a van, and that was when the firing started. Bullets flew all around us, coming for our heads and our bodies. There was no escaping them. We tried to dodge them by lowering our bodies as we scattered everywhere, running home, running into people's homes to seek shelter. People hit the ground with blood on their backs. We ran into one other, our bodies colliding. Blood was spewing all around me and I had my white shirt to show for it. Some old people nearby who had been sitting in the sun or under trees ran indoors for shelter. Many people refused to open their doors because they feared the police might come to their homes. It was a disaster. Some people were struck by bullets while they were in their homes, not because they were out there with us. We just fled and kept going and going, unsure of where we were headed.

15

I WAS RUNNING with the feeling that at any second my body would hit the ground because there were bullets coming for me. It was terrifying. I was not even sure of where to run to, home was very far away. My legs jumped fences with almost the same speed as they ran. My already dry and sore throat was made worse by the running and I wanted to stop, but I knew that hiding behind someone's house was not safe enough. I thought my legs would give in because I could hardly feel them anymore. Frantically, I knocked on someone's door and begged them to let me in, screaming. But no one answered. People were too afraid.

Desperate to be inside, I climbed up the wall and, balancing one foot on a faucet, pushed myself through the bathroom window. I had no idea whose house it was, nor did I care. Shielding my head with both arms, I fell head first onto the floor. I thought I had broken my arm. All of my limbs ached and I could hardly breathe, my chest felt parched from the dust, the tear gas, and the running. My shoulder hurt a lot from the fall. It was impossible to say which part of me hurt the most. I just ached everywhere as I lay there, all out of breadth. My eyes stung from the gas and I kept blinking and trying to see what was around me, but I had to shut them tightly to alleviate the pain. I lay motionless on that floor for what felt like forever, until a small, elderly woman came and stood at the door. She gave me a fright, but I did not scream or move because I had no strength to do either. I could hardly lift my head to see her face, and so I lay there and squinted and looked at her feet and cane. For a minute she seemed more afraid of me than I was of her because she had her walking stick pointed at my face, as if ready to strike if a made a move. When I finally managed to raise my eyes to her face, both of us just stared at each other for a while without saying a word.

"Whose child are you?" she asked, almost whispering. She too must have been afraid of being heard from outside. I started to move my lips but no voice came out. I tried again but nothing happened. She moved closer to me and I rolled over and lay on my back so that I could look up at her without having to lift my head. I did not feel any more trusting towards her than she did towards me. My concern was that she would call the police out of fright.

"What is wrong with your voice?" she asked, and still my lips moved, but there was no voice. I kept thinking that she would find me more suspicious if I did not say a word to her, and it became more and more crucial that I reassure her. My head felt faint and I had to will myself not to pass out, fearing that she would call someone to take me to the hospital, which would put me right into the hands of the police. I was sure that they were out there still looking for victims, and that if I came out they would take one look at my school uniform and I would be in detention before the day was over. My mother would come home from work and not know where on earth I was. I did not know this woman and she had no idea what family I belonged to, so she may not tell the right people.

All these thoughts kept me alert and my head racing. The woman said, "Can you stand up?" and to my surprise, I could pull my body up, perhaps it was out of fear. "Good, because I don't have that kind of strength anymore."

She motioned with her hand for me to follow her. My feet felt heavy and my legs felt wobbly as I walked behind her. Although she needed a walking stick, I moved a lot slower than she did. I held on to the walls until I got to the kitchen, still feeling paranoid and thinking that the men in green uniform may still be out there waiting and watching. I was dizzy and felt so faint, I thought I would fall back down at any minute.

The woman told me to sit down as she leaned over the stove,

making something that smelled like ginger. She walked to the fridge and took out a container full of water and then proceeded to pour me some of it in a large, round cup. I drank it like I was inhaling a breath of fresh air. I was so quick that she had to tell me to slow down, warning me that I could swallow it down the wrong passage. She sat across the table from me, watching. My head was less dizzy after the cup of water, and I allowed myself to rest it against the wall behind me, trusting the stranger a little.

"Thank you," I managed to say.

"Whose child are you?" the woman asked. That was probably the most important question for her at that time, because it would help her determine which neighbour she needed to notify. Either that or it would determine her degree of sympathy. If I belonged to a family she knew well she might feel sorry for my mother.

"My mother is Kgomotso Masimo."

"Up near Martha?" she asked, referring to my neighbour.

I nodded.

"Where is Kgomotso now, at work?"

I nodded again. I needed to keep my eyes closed because they still hurt from the gas. It felt rude not to be looking at her or giving answers with words, but it was too difficult to stay focused. It was hard because she seemed so desperate to have some answers from me.

"Your sister is Keitumetse, right?"

Again I nodded, but this time her question sent me into another panic. My sister had not been at the march because she was still not able to leave the house. I realized that I had to phone her and let her know I was fine. By now she would have heard about the shootings and would be wondering where I was.

"Do you have a phone?" I asked suddenly, and my voice startled the woman.

"Yes. But I locked it. My grandchildren play with the phone. The bills are too high." She had stood up and was on her way out of the kitchen as she said this, and I stumbled behind her.

The phone rang only once before Keitumetse picked it up.

"Don't come home, there are police vans all over this street," she warned me. "Also, they came in here asking me questions about the headquarters."

"They know about that?" I asked, my voice still sounding low.

"No, but they want to know where all of this started, so they will probably find out. Don't go there either."

My sister must have just been relieved to hear that I was fine because she forgot to ask where I was. I promised her I would not go home, but evaded the question of whether or not I would be going to the office.

"Tihelo," she said softly, and my heart pounded because I knew it was something awful. "They killed Thabang. Did you hear?"

I just stood there frozen, not really thinking anything, just stunned.

"Tihelo?" she said, and sounded like she was about to cry.

"I'll come home when I think it's safe," I said and hung up the phone, not ready to feel upset or think about what she had told me. Somehow I had to find my way to the headquarters because I suddenly realized that there was a lot of work to do. I could barely move from one room to another, so I knew I would find it difficult to make my way to the SASO office. The elderly woman, whose name I still did not know because there was hardly any polite way of asking, sat on a sofa across from me looking concerned.

"I have to leave," I told her.

"With those feet?"

"I really have to go somewhere," I said

"Let's soak those feet in warm water first," she said and then got up and went to the kitchen. I felt so restless that I thought she was moving too slowly. I became very impatient. But she called out to me from the kitchen, saying I should come and soak my legs.

In front of the chair I had been sitting in before, she had filled a small round container with warm water and some of what she had been cooking on the stove. Although I still felt impatient, her gestures felt warm and caring and I tried to slow myself down enough to sit on the chair for a few minutes. I took off my shoes and socks and put my aching feet in the warm, ginger-smelling water, which was immediately soothing.

For a few minutes we sat there together quietly. I enjoyed feeling the warmth of the water and taking in the smell of the ginger and both of us drank some tea that she had just made. She kept telling me to stay away from the police, to go to school and become something.

"These children are walking right into the mouth of the lion with their marching and rioting," she said. I was not feeling completely rested and her words made me more and more nervous. I had so much to do at the headquarters and I had to find a way out of there.

"You should take off that uniform if you don't want them to see you," she said. "I have something you can wear."

I was a little bit stunned at what she presented me with: a very long red dress, a pair of high heels, a wig, and a handbag. She said, "They are my daughter's clothes, and the wig is mine. You have to promise to bring them back, otherwise I won't let you take them."

I promised.

"I used to wear that in 1958, when I was still young," she said, pointing proudly at the wig. I thought it was a little bit amusing, considering she did not look like she would have been that young in 1958. I thought she would probably have been in her forties.

The high heels were daunting. My feet felt quite a bit better, but I had never put on a pair of high-heel shoes in my entire fourteen years of living.

Time was flying and I had to be back at the headquarters as soon as possible. So I changed into my borrowed clothes and, as terrified as I was of going back into the streets, I thanked the woman profusely and hurried out. The entire time I tried to look like I knew what I was doing, but the heels were painful. As I passed the vans and hippos patrolling the neighbourhoods, I wondered if I really looked as ridiculous as I felt. I was positive that at any minute a police officer would recognize me from the protest and put me in a van. My eyes were on the ground and on my shoes, I would not have dared to make eye contact with anyone—policeman or civilian. My feet were retluctant to take me far, but I persisted. What I had to do was urgent and crucial.

When I finally reached the headquarters, I thought for the first time about how there could be policemen guarding the place, and how I had not considered that before I came. My carelessness scared me, made me think of what might happen next time I did not take time to consider everything before making a move. But there was no one there. I could not help but marvel at how the comrades had managed to keep the place a secret for so long—longer than I knew. But even I was aware that it would only be a matter of time before they found it, which was why I had to be swift. This time I had keys, since I had been working with Dikeledi in the winter. I tried to look like an ordinary woman coming home from work and going into her house, even though I knew that if someone were watching me, I would be in jail for eternity.

As soon as I got inside, I took off the heels and went straight to the recorded material. I thought the pamphlets were not so important, they could wait. The tapes and books had to go first because not only were they banned and considered to be some of the most incriminating things you could have in your possession in the country, but they were also the most precious and rare things we had in that house. There were recordings of speeches given by Mandela, Sisulu, Tambo, and Biko, of whom three were in jail and one was dead. They were things we did not want to lose. Someone's schoolbag was on the floor in the front room, so I took the tapes and books and tried to fit as many of them in there as I could. The rest I put in a large plastic bag, but I realized that it would be impossible to take everything. All that time I had to use a candle because it was getting dark outside and I could barely see. Turning on the lights would have been too dangerous, because after I left no one would probably be coming for a while. If anyone had been watching, they would think it strange that the light had been on for less than an hour the whole evening. I was trying to be careful about everything, doing my best not to raise too many eyebrows.

Every time I thought of Thabang, Tshepo, or Dikeledi, I forced myself to think of something else I had to do. I would start talking to myself, saying things like: "What else? What else are you forgetting?" Then when that got old, I started thinking of jokes I had heard recently, maybe even something I had heard from Lebo. It was a little game I played with myself. I tried to think of as many things as possible that could distract me. Allowing myself to think of the comrades and the massacre would be too upsetting and I would not get anything done, so I would do things like count backwards from a hundred to one. I would picture cars and try to remember their names, think of historical facts and say them out loud. It was not an easy task, taking everything people, including myself, had worked on for months and months, things that were still needed and could still be of use, and deciding which way to dispose of them.

I took the pamphlets, the posters, the paintings, and the T-shirts, scooped them in my arms, and threw as many as I could in the kitchen sink. I went to the bathroom and flushed away whatever I thought would go down the drain quickly, mostly pieces of paper. The things that I could not flush I put in the kitchen sink and set alight. One of the hardest part was deciding to burn books, and burning Tshepo's art was heartbreaking. I saw some of Thabang's writings too and had to get rid of them. As excruciating as it was, I had to work very swiftly and had no time to stop and mourn.

I went around the house looking to see if there was any incriminating evidence left. All that time my feet ached so badly that I flinched with almost every step I took. I could not imagine walking home, but I would not even consider sleeping alone at the headquarters because it was too dangerous. There was not telling how long it would take the police to find the place.

In the end I could not really carry the bag that I had filled with tapes and books. Not only would it be impossible to walk in those shoes and carry a heavy bag, but I was well aware of how suspicious I might look—a working woman in high heels with an extra large school bag. The only thing that made sense was to take the material I thought most important—a decision that was almost impossible to make—and put it in the handbag. But only a few tapes would fit, so I filled two large plastic bags and carried them like I was bringing home groceries from OK and Checkers. Finally, forcing myself not to think too much about what I was doing, and trying not to look back too many times, I closed the doors of the house and went out through the front. I thought it best not to sneak around behind people's houses because it would make me look suspicious. Also, I was trying not to feel too frightened. I needed to stop constantly looking behind my back and hoping that no one saw me. If I walked the streets like anyone else then I would feel less like I was drawing too much attention to myself. My plan was that if anyone asked where I was going after dark then I would tell them I was going home to my children. I only hoped that I looked old enough to pass for a very mature teenage mother.

16

I WALKED ALONGSIDE men and women who were just returning home from work, and I chatted with them to make myself feel less nervous. Some people wondered who I was; someone even spoke Afrikaans to me because with my very light skin under the straight auburn hair of the wig I looked Coloured. I thought it was rather amusing.

The women and men I walked among were talking about the massacre that had taken place that afternoon. They wondered if their children would be there when they arrived home, and they asked me if I knew anything about what had happened that afternoon.

"I'm going home just like you," I lied. "But I did hear about it on the radio in the taxi."

"You know, you go to work in the morning and your worst fear is that they will be in detention or have disappeared when you come back," one woman, who looked older than most, said with sadness in her voice. "But you never really realize, that's not the worst that could happen."

The other women shook their heads and clicked their tongues, acknowledging what a tragedy had happened that afternoon. One man said he knew his son was really active in the struggle, and that he hoped that afternoon had been different.

"Maybe he decided to stay home or something," he said, hoping out loud. I watched him turn the corner and walk home with the Checkers bag full of groceries and wondered whose father he was. It was too painful to ask the women, considering there was a good chance that I might know his son, and I did not want to have one more name to block out of my mind.

✳

I arrived home safely. Most of the streetlamps had been turned off and I was thankful to have had companions on my way. Lights in people's homes were not on either. In the candlelit kitchen my mother sat at the table with my sister, who looked more alert than she had in months. They both stood up, relieved to see me.

"*Iyoo,* Tihelo!" Keitumetse cried. "Where have you been?!"

"It was hard coming home, I had to wait a long time until it felt safe enough."

"What are you wearing?" my mother exclaimed, slightly amused.

"I was hiding in an old woman's house and she gave me her clothes. My school uniform would have looked too obvious." They both nodded, understanding.

"What is in the bags?" Mama asked

I hesitated to tell them, but I knew there was no use in hiding anything. So I explained my reasoning and why I thought it was necessary to go to the headquarters and destroy everything that I could. Keitumetse found it really disturbing that I had done that because she thought my actions marked the end of the office and everything in it. Mama was more concerned about the parents of the students who had been killed.

"Thabang's mother works in the kitchens, she probably will not be home for another day or two," she told us. "They sent her brother, Thabang's uncle, to tell her."

"Do you know anyone else who was killed or hurt?" I asked cautiously, and my sister shook her head.

"Mapitse's son was also killed, I met her on my way home from work just after she had heard the news," my mother informed us. I was numb. I just sat there and stared at her with my mouth wide open. Peter was dead? Peter, my childhood friend and neighbour? I had no tears. Nor did I wish I could cry. My body had reverted to that state where all the hard emotions were tied up in a knot inside it. It felt like it was the end of the world.

"You two have to stay strong and know that we will probably be hearing about a lot more people. I don't want you to fall apart," my mother said sternly. "There will be a lot of deaths to deal with and people's families will need our help and support. Tihelo, people's parents might ask you questions about their children because you were there."

"What kinds of questions?" I was afraid.

"Well, like what role their children played in the organizing of this march," she said.

"Or if you saw them get shot," Keitumetse added.

"Well, I don't think I saw anyone I know get shot, a lot of bodies that I saw were lying face down. I really cannot say I saw anyone I can identify. I was too busy running for shelter."

"This is not what we are asking you. We thought we should tell you what to expect from other parents," my mother said. "Don't panic, *ngwanake*, just tell people how good and courageous their children were, that is really all they will be hoping to hear. When people die we want to hear only the best things about them. You might be just the person to tell everyone what they need to hear, that's all."

Although we were constantly worried about them, Keitumetse and I were relieved that Tshepo and Mohau were not in the country. Who knew where they would be at this point, if they had been in the township that afternoon? We knew Mohau would have probably been where Thabang had been, he probably would have been the one leading the crowd and stepping up to the podium to make our demands heard. When I thought about that I allowed myself for the first time to wonder what had happened to Dikeledi. Although both Keitumetse and Mama had told me about two dead comrades, I knew they had names, but I would not ask who else was fatally wounded, just in case it was someone whose face and voice I could recall easily.

My sister and I spent the night in our mother's bed, lying on our backs and letting the cold air from the outside slip through our nightgowns and hit our bare skin. All three of us were extremely tired, both physically and emotionally. We heard gunshots, but none of us flinched the way one should when that kind of noise is in your neighbourhood. We just lay there and listened to our bodies without saying a single word to each other for hours. Eventually I began to drift in and out of sleep, waking up whenever I heard Thabang's voice in my dreams. It was loud and heavy and I had to extricate myself from its grip every time it came and took hold of me. It may have been that my body was recalling the day's events, but it was also possible that guilt was gnawing at my heart, telling me I should have been closer to the front. I felt like a coward—I wondered if I had consciously stood right in the middle, where it was harder for the police to see me.

Every time I woke up I startled either my mother or my sister from their sleep. Mama had to put her hand on my chest and rub it two or three times during the night, because I woke up sobbing and my chest heaving. After a while I just opened my eyes and willed them to stay open. I wanted to go through the tapes and books to distract myself, but I knew that getting out of bed would wake up my family and only make them more worried.

I just lay there staring at the curtains billowing towards the ceiling as the wind blew them in, waiting desperately for the sun to come up. It was difficult not to be able to fall asleep because I had hoped that it would take me away from the day's events. Instead, all it did was take me closer and closer to the scene of the massacre. Faces of people I knew came at me as soon as I closed my eyes, and I had to lift my head off the pillow every time my mind gave in to the seductiveness of sleep. The events—the shooting, the sound of a hippo about to bulldoze people into the ground in broad daylight, people's shrieks—were all in my head, sitting comfortably and waiting for me to doze off. As long as I stayed awake I managed to avoid them. It was so unbearable that about two hours before dawn I woke my mother up and asked her to talk to me.

I allowed myself to ask for comfort. It was an unusual moment for both of us, just like the time I had cried on her lap when Keitumetse was in the hospital. It felt private and intimate as if it was just the two of us, even though my sister was sleeping on the other side of me. I asked Mama questions to keep both of us awake.

"Are you going to work tomorrow?" I asked.

"Yes, I have to." she responded, but she did not look awake enough. I wanted to keep her interested.

I asked her about my grandmother, whom I had only known for the first five years of my life. I held on to my mother's arm with both my hands, gripping it tightly as she told me about her mother. I kept moving closer and closer, pressing my body against hers, desperate for comfort. When she spoke, I concentrated really hard and took in every word. She answered every question patiently as we lay there whispering to each other, while she stroked my hair and kissed my forehead. She was fully aware of my anguish and of the fact that I was asking questions to keep myself from feeling it all. We could not clearly see each other's faces at that time of night, and so we relied solely on each other's voices to tell us how the other person was feeling.

"Was she tall, like you?" I asked

"Yes, and very light-skinned, like you." I had never heard that before, and it made me feel an overwhelming sense of stability, something that up to that point I had never felt so easily. I remembered for the first time in a long time the thoughts I used to have when I was younger, before I went to high school. The things that had stayed in my mind and terrified me, everything I had never had the audacity to mention them to my family. Questions like, "What if one day someone comes for me and says I belong to them?" and "What if no one knows where I really came from?" and "What if my mother wondered whether I had been switched at birth at the hospital and she had got the wrong baby?" Some of these musings were the stuff of American television dramas—they were silly, but they still had me wondering. I had the kinds of questions that would only make sense to a mind filled with fear. Or that would only seem logical in extreme heat, when your head has been in the sun for longer than any part of your body should be, without any kind of shield from the rays. As I lay there with my mother, thinking about those questions, I smiled slightly at how ridiculous they were.

"What else?" I asked

"She knew her history like the palm of her hand."

"Like me."

"Like you," she said. "My mother knew facts about parts of the world that I had never even heard of. She knew about women's lives in faraway lands, about wars fought in ancient countries. She knew everything, all you had to do was ask her."

"Mama?" I asked

"Hmmm??"

"Tell me about our father."

After I said it she paused for a while before saying anything. I thought I had upset her, but when she finally spoke she said, "I loved him very much." And I knew from her voice that she really had nothing else to say, at least for that moment. It would be my last quiet moment with my mother for a very long time.

17

BY THE TIME MORNING came, the two of us were sleeping like babies. It was a Saturday morning and for the first time in many months, Mama had not woken up to go to work. We were soon to find out that almost none of the parents in the neighbourhood had. They had decided it was time to take over what we had started, they were going out on the streets and to protest the mass murder we had just witnessed.

The entire township was a disaster area. Mothers and fathers were knocking on people's doors, asking every parent to take part in a demonstration to protest against police brutality. Mama asked my sister and I to stay home and not open the doors to anyone except her. We stayed home in a panic and watched her leave the house with a group of women and men from our street. Because Peter's mother was in mourning, she was supposed to sit on a bare mattress in her home, but she appeared at our back door waiting for my mother to come and join her in the demonstration. It was the protest our parents had hoped all their lives never to have to take part in—we had all hoped for so long that this would not come to pass where we lived. People our parents' age were still feeling shock at, and had not recovered from, the 1976 massacre of students or the Sharpville bloodbath of 1960. Althought those had been the two bigger and best-remembered massacres, we knew that people were killed by the police in smaller groups several times a year, in different parts of the country.

No matter how horrified we were, for us, the children of this township, this was our first major massacre. Our parents had lived through many more, and wherever they had been when previous tragedies happened, the entire Black population had mourned. I wondered whether our fellow comrades would walk their streets in different parts of the country to protest the deaths of their friends. Keitumetse said that she had the feeling people would be marching even outside the country. We had to remember that the ANC had support everywhere, and a lot of the people in exile were constantly organizing rallies and telling the world about what was going on in South Africa. We both thought of Mohau and Tshepo, and wondered out loud whether or not they had any idea who had died.

"Mohau will probably know soon if he doesn't already," Keitumetse told me.

"I was just wondering if I should try and contact comrades in Soweto, but I think that would be too risky," I told Keitumetse.

"Well, you know how fast people move. Contacts are everywhere. I would be surprised if the names of all who were killed have not been released to everyone who should know."

"Keitumetse," I started to ask in an even lower tone, "what does Mohau say?"

My sister hesitated, wrinkling her forehead. "Just that he is fine, and he and Tshepo are with good comrades. They miss home and cannot send messages to their family because the police are constantly watching their homes. It would put their family in danger."

"They're watching their family? Their grandparents?"

Keitumetse nodded.

We were talking in the living room, watching different groups of parents walk past in a hurry, rushing to the meeting point. It was a dark and eerie morning; it felt like we had moved into the middle of a quiet winter night. Even though most people were enraged, there was hardly any noise. I noticed how the adults did things very differently compared to us. We started singing and marching as soon as we stepped into the streets. There was no meeting point; we just had people join us as we went along. With them there was no running or dancing. Women hugged their bodies the way they usually did when they were going to pay their respects to a mourning family.

The police were still all over the township, doing things to aggravate us, like flying helicopters over our houses. Every tactic they used was for the purpose of intimidating us, warning us to either stay home or deal with the consequences. We just wanted the nightmare to come to an end. Our parents marched to demand an end to all the violence, the mass detentions, and the state of emergency. We needed to be able to come home and switch on the lights for as long as we wanted to. We wanted to walk freely on our own streets. We wanted to end the fear. But the police had other ideas. They needed to put us neatly in our houses where they could see us, and not out on the streets where they could not keep track of where we all were. The government sent out their trained soldiers, other people's children, to come and keep us in order. Those other people—the ones whose children were coming at us with deadly force—were out in their homes where they sat and enjoyed lemonade or cola in the sun. Although they may have been worried about their children's safety, they were positive their children were heroes. Their children were seen as soldiers of peace, serving a country they had come to call their own. They were doing what they could to protect their *"vaderland"* from the grips of the "natives." These soldiers thought they were defending themselves from us, from these places we lived in—places that their mothers and fathers had created for us. But these were places we ourselves were struggling to protect ourselves from. We lived every day dreaming of safer homes and gun-free streets.

So we watched our mothers and fathers go out that dusky Saturday morning, lashing out at the world in our defence. We had been asked to stay home and not say a word because it was their turn to be out there on our behalf. In all the time that I had known her, my mother had never participated in a demonstration. Her work and her quiet disposition had probably kept her from saying what she needed to. I knew she was frustrated by everything that was going on because she spoke to me about it. She had told me things I would never forget, things that I did not understand so well when I was younger, but that I had grown to fully comprehend. But it must have been too much for her to watch me come home the night before in someone else's clothes, barely able to stand, both my sister and I already having so many people to mourn in our early teens.

All day Keitumetse and I had had been receiving telephone calls from friends trying to see if the two of us were fine. Neighbours were in and out of the house—we let them in even though we were not supposed to. They came to show their concern. Some people had questions about who had died and who had survived, some had news and had phoned to tell us what they knew. I found it really difficult to speak to everyone without thinking I was going to be sick. My hands were shaky all day and so were my legs. Finally, after one phone call from a schoolfriend telling me Lebo had been wounded and was in the hospital, I asked Keitumetse to let the phone ring. There was only so much I could hear in one day. But just as we thought we had shut out all surprises for the day, we opened the door to a long-lost friend—Thato.

She came knocking at our door that afternoon, looking a lot less distressed than most people we had seen that day, but still upset. Keitumetse opened the door and invited her in, but she asked my sister to sit outside on the *stoep* with her. I was in the bedroom lying on my bed when I heard her greet my sister, and I was too stunned to get up. Keitumetse called me, and I took my time going outside because I was too busy trying to decide how to act when I saw her.

When I finally did go outside, I tried to seem as composed as possible. She was sitting next to my sister, her hair long and straight and falling down to her shoulders. It was so pretty that it made me stare for a moment. She took about five seconds to turn around and look at me when I came, and even then she did not look me in the eye.

"Hello," I said.

"Hi," she said smoothly. No one said "hi" around here.

Keitumetse sensed the awkwardness between us, so she took over the conversation.

"Thato just said her parents' store was looted last night."

"Why?" I was quite shocked because her parents had so much respect from the community. I thought that it must have been because of the post-massacre rage.

"I think they did it to every shop around here," Thato said in Setswana. This took me by surprise because from what I remembered she almost never spoke the language anymore.

"I think people were really infuriated by everything the police did," I said in defence of people I probably knew.

"Why did they march?" Thato asked, and for the first time in a long time, I did not care much about what she thought because she seemed really unaware of everything going on around her.

"We," I said, and she wrinkled her forehead slightly with surprise, and then nodded. "We need answers about where people are, so many people have been detained that we don't know where half our friends are anymore."

I obviously made her uncomfortable speaking like that. She made an indirect statement by asking me a question and looking me straight in the eye for the first time.

"Where is Tshepo?" she asked with suppressed anger. I resented her implication that I was being "taken in" by comrades. I knew she was thinking this because I remembered our reactions when we thought Tshepo was putting his life at risk unnecessarily. My first instinct was to tell her she knew so little that it was sad. Then I wanted her to keep running in the same direction that she had started going when she went to a multiracial school. I wanted to say: Get away while you can, you don't need any of this! But then I was also quite angry with her question, feeling like she really undermined what I had been going through since I started high school.

"He's safe," I said, looking right back at her. She rolled her eyes and I almost started yelling at her, but Keitumetse intervened.

"*Sho!* I'm sure your parents will be okay. Did they go to the march?"

"Hmmm," Thato said, nodding her head.

"Tihelo, maybe we should get Thato a cold drink," my sister said.

"We don't have any," I responded

"Well, I'll go and buy some," she said.

Thato stood up and said, "No, there's no one in the house and I should get back."

"No, you haven't visited in a long time. I'll get us a cold drink and then you can go," Keitumetse said, and then got up and left.

"Your parents both went?" I asked Thato when we were alone. We both felt awkward and unsure of what to say to each other.

"*Ja,*" she responded. We both sat looking at nothing.

"How is school?" I asked again

"School is okay," she said.

"Do you have a lot of friends?" My hurt and resentment got the better of me and I just had to ask, bitterly.

She nodded and responded with a no, which I thought was probably an attempt to make me feel less resentful. We stared in front of us without saying a word to each other, but both of us sensed the unbearable tension. By the time Keitumetse came back, I was ready to go back to my room and I could sense that Thato was ready to go home. But we sat there for a while longer, talking about our parents and the march, until Thato made a swift exit. I felt like we had talked about something there, but I was not sure what that was.

My mother returned with a few other women from the neighbourhood. They all looked so distraught that I could hardly bring myself to ask what had happened. Mama came to sit between my sister and me, hugging her body tightly as if to comfort herself. When she told us that they had not come back with more news than they had had when they left, I was disappointed because I had hoped that their quieter demonstration would carry more weight. But in spite of that, I felt a great sense of relief because nothing worse had happened. They had gone and stood in front of the police office, at that same spot where we had been the day before, but nothing happened. They had said what they needed to say and gone home in the late afternoon without answers. Those who were hoping to come back with their children got nothing, and perhaps those who had already lost their children felt a little worse as they stood in that bloodied spot wondering which stain was their children's blood. Maybe it felt especially distressing for them to go there and stand up for their children's innocence a day too late. But no one came home feeling any more powerful than before. It had been draining for everyone; our spirits were all down.

For the rest of the evening Mama acted really apologetic, looking at Keitumetse and me like she owed us the world. We sat and ate together, and I thought about how much better my sister looked. Her eyes no longer made her look as if she was still recovering from something awful. There was so much going on around us, with police vans speeding through quiet streets, and gunshots going off so loud and so close that it was hard not to think someone had fired the gun right in our backyard. But it was comforting to have survived what was probably our township's greatest tragedy to date. My family was all under one roof and Mama told us to recognize how lucky that was.

"They had no reason at all to kill those children. There is no reason for us to think it couldn't have happened to any of us," Mama said. "And today . . . today . . . they tried some of the same things they did with you yesterday. They joked and laughed and spat at us. It was all to intimidate us, firing guns in the air . . . all of that was to say we are nothing. They feel there's no reason to even pay a little attention to us."

"Mama did you see the newspaper today?" I asked.

"Yes, someone had it at the demonstration. I know, I know."

"What?" Keitumetse asked.

"Well," Mama said, taking a deep breath. "The *Sowetan* reported the massacre on the front page, but the White newspapers had nothing about it. I know one paper had a brief report about it on, I think, page ten or something. The front page of one other paper had a White man lying on a beach . . . something about early vacations."

None of us had anything to say to that. I stood up to put my plate in the sink.

"Tlhelo," Mama said, "I put away your books and papers." I panicked at that because I had been too preoccupied to remember placing them in a safe place. There was my carelessness again. I was amazed at myself.

"Thank you. Where did you put them?" I asked

"I took them out of the house," Mama said, turning to plat Keitumetse's hair and not looking up at me. I was stunned at her cavalier attitude and my face must have given away what I was feeling because she added something. "They are a lot safer where I put them," she said, and refused to tell me where that was.

I sat down and watched her platting my sister's hair. My mind kept going back to the massacre, and I sat there forcing myself to concentrate on my sister's hair being neatly parted and braided. I thought really hard about my mother's hands, her large palms and their long, slender fingers. Her face looked tired but focused even when she occasionally turned to look at me.

"Tihelo, where is Dikeledi?" Keitumetse pulled me away from my focus.

"I don't know. I don't want to go to her house in case it is being watched. She also spoke up at the gathering. She was standing next to Thabang, but I really don't know if she was wounded." It was still hard to say "killed." I could not use that word about anyone at all.

"If you call the hospital they might tell you."

"I don't think I'll call," I said

"Sometimes the police ask the nurses to watch who comes to visit patients," Mama said. "This time they will be looking out for people they saw at the protest. They hope to find people who might lead them to more information," Mama said. "So both of you should stay home. Don't go anywhere near that hospital."

"Mama, do you think school will reopen?" Keitumetse asked under Mama's hands.

"I hope so. But I know there will not be a lot of people willing to go if it does open," I responded.

"Tihelo, I want you to go to school when it does open," Mama said.

"I will go. I don't want to, but I will. No one will be there, Mama."

"We will see what happens."

"Mama, was it exactly like this when you went to school?" I asked.

"It was a lot like this. Apartheid was made law the year that I was born, but protests had been going on long before I was even born. I remember Sharpeville, June 1976, and Biko's death. You were here for some of it. Do you remember anything?"

"I think so. I remember the riots after Soweto and I remember when Biko died. I was seven."

19

IN THE MIDDLE OF the night as I fought off images of people's bodies hitting the ground, our kitchen door burst open under the forceful pressure of a steel boot. I heard dogs barking loudly in our backyard and then they were in our kitchen. My mother's bedroom was suddenly flooded with lights from what felt like hundreds of blinding flashlights. The three of us were in bed and we screamed and struggled to resist the grips of men in uniform, strangers who had let themselves in. They handcuffed us and pulled us out one at a time, pushing us forward with kicks of their steel boots. They yelled in our ears, mouths wide open and so close that I thought I could see their little tongues flickering in their throats as they screamed profanities. I kept turning my head away from them but they were all around me. My mind told me that they would either spit at me or bite off my nose. My feet were very cold and I begged them to at least let me put on my shoes, while my mother yelled at them to just let us stay.

"*Kom! kom!*" they said. My mother repeatedly kicked and hit out at them, and begged them to take her and leave her children, but they just pulled us out of our house barefoot and barely clothed. Someone got sick of my mother's screams and hit her with the handle of a large pistol. She arched her back and almost fell face down, but they were quick to catch her.

Someone asked which one of us was Tihelo, and someone else said it made no difference.

"*Uit! Uit! Kom!*" They pushed us out, telling us to hurry, that we were wasting their time. They took us out through our front door and I saw that all the neighbours had switched on their lights, standing out on their front *stoeps* and their gates watching.

A neighbour yelled out, "We will come and get you, Mma Tihelo!" I thought that probably every van they had at the police station was out there waiting with deadly weapons for this seemingly dangerous person called Tihelo. A person they obviously had never met or seen.

I knew that someone must have said something about me being a member of the SASO. This could not be a result of someone spotting me at the protest march in front of the police station. But my mind was driving me insane because I kept thinking that maybe the man high up in the hippo that had come for me at the protest had a really good memory. Maybe he had sent them, I thought even though I realized that made no sense at all.

My wrists felt as if the handcuffs were cutting them, they were so painful. "You are going to be sorry for everything you've been doing!" a man in uniform yelled out in English, but with an Afrikaans accent. His voice sounded heavier than the words, which he spoke from his throat.

When we reached the gate I could not even see my family; I could only hear their screams. Keitumetse was just crying, not cursing them out, which is what the neighbours were doing. Someone's boot stepped on my foot and I let out a shriek. The man then responded by hitting his large palm against the back of my head, his way of telling me to shut up.

Finally they pushed us into the back of a green van. I thought that I must be having one of my nightmares. As the car raced through the township my sister cried on my mother's shoulder, but Mama could not hold her because she was also handcuffed. People outside yelled at the police, calling them dogs. We were not the only ones who were enraged.

"Some of them probably stayed and searched the house. Is there anything in there that you're worried about?" My mother asked me.

"I don't know what they would think was illegal. I never brought things home, I hope they don't find—"

"They won't." She reassured me about the tapes and books without actually saying the words.

We had no idea where we were going in that van. I wondered if they would take us all to the same place, since I knew they did not often put family or friends together. My biggest worry was that they would separate us. I did not care about what they would do with us, just as long as they kept us together. My hands were beginning to feel numb and I had to keep shaking them and stretching my fingers. I could not cry the way Keitumetse could, I thought that if I started I would never stop. My mother kept asking me if I was okay and I kept telling her that I was. We were all really uncomfortable in there but I did not complain. There was a strong stench in the back of the van. It was frustrating to be in it for so long.

What was happening to us felt familiar, even though I had never experienced it before. I remembered when I still had very little knowledge of what was going on around us, when the police would come and take men and women and put them in the back of their vans and then drive them around the township looking for more people. Sometimes a green van would be parked outside of someone's house and I would walk by and see faces, eyes peering out through the windows with the fencelike covering that made it hard to recognize who was in there. I had found the eyes really frightening and thought of the people as outlaws, people who had done something that I did not want to know about. I was afraid first of the van itself and second of the people inside. That night as my mother, my sister, and I rode away I was thankful that it was not happening in broad daylight. I would not have liked to be seen by a little girl. I would have hated for my face to be the source of her nightmares.

We rode for longer than I could bear, unsure of where we were going, what we were being detained for, or who was in the front seat driving us. I had a pounding headache from the palm of a man whose face I had not seen. My mother said her back was aching, and my sister kept asking where we were going between bouts of sobbing. At first we assumed that we would be taken to the local prison, near where the students and my fellow comrades had recently been killed, but the ride became too long so we thought we were probably on our way to Pretoria.

"There'll be more White policemen there," my mother said with regret in her voice. It took me a minute to remember that she had spent a night in that same place not so long ago.

"Okay. Tihelo, Keitumetse, listen to me," Mama started, and my heart sank. "We might not be put together if they hold us for more than one night. So I want the two of you to listen to me very carefully."

I felt so nervous and uncomfortable that I closed my eyes really tight and braced myself for her words. Keitumetse shifted her weight a little as if to give my mother some room, and kept sniffling and crying, she was so distraught.

"No matter what they say to you and no matter what they do to you, just keep saying you don't know anything. They will probably ask you and Keitumetse about where Mohau is. If you are losing strength, lie," she whispered. Neither of us could say anything, we were so afraid. "Tihelo, try to sound your age. I know you've done a lot and you know a lot more than even your sister about what's been going on around here, but you have to act as if you're too young to know anything. In case someone saw you at the protest march, just say you were in school and people demanded that you join them. Act like you are just an innocent child, not a comrade. Otherwise they could lock you up for a very long time."

I was taking deep breaths to calm myself while she spoke. I did not realize how loud my sister's crying had been until that moment when my mother stopped speaking and the only noise we could hear was the sound of the van's engine and cars driving past.

"And," my mother began, and my headache got worse. She paused a moment and took a deep breath. "If they do something to us, if we don't see each other again, I want you both to know that you are my girls and I love you both very, very much. Don't believe anything else they tell you."

"Like what?" I asked, suddenly confused. "What would they tell us?"

"Sometimes they tell people that their families have moved and left them. If they let me out I will go home; I am not going anywhere without you. Other times they will tell you that your family confessed and gave them information about you. They will say that just to get you to admit things to them. Don't admit anything, even if they give you the names of the comrades you know well and make you think that your friends have spoken to the police. It's always a lie. No comrade ever tells them anything. Tihelo . . ." She stopped after saying my name and took a deep breadth, but did not look at me. "I suspect they may keep you longer because they are looking for comrades. I suspect they will let Keitumetse and me go, but I'm not sure. If they do, they may also never let us see you. If that happens, know that we did come. We will be coming every day to see you."

I felt like she was saying goodbye to me, like she was giving me up. My head kept pounding, and I felt worse and worse. I was angry with myself for going back to the headquarters and working again, thinking that I should have stayed home and remained uninvolved. All kinds of regrets raced through me. I wondered who would go and demand my release at the jail gates now that my friends and comrades were either dead, detained, disappeared, or in exile. Pure fear was consuming me in that van; I had no empowering thoughts whatsoever. Thinking of what I was doing at the SASO offices was no help because it only brought back memories of people I preferred not to think about at that point. I may have felt before like I could defeat the powers that be, but those thoughts were nowhere near me that night. It was pure hell.

My nightgown was too flimsy for the cold coming though the fencelike shield. All of us said our feet were freezing. Our powerlessness was frustrating. We had no idea what they would do with us once we got there, if they were going to let us live or not. We would have liked to have been able to hug each other, both for comfort and for warmth, but our hands were tied tightly behind our backs. I kept wondering whether or not I would see someone in jail I knew, maybe a long-lost neighbour or a friend who had just disappeared without a trace. My mother was looking down, her chin on her chest, and she seemed more distraught after speaking to us. I shifted my body closer to her and put my head on her shoulder, and she turned her head so that it rested on mine. Keitumetse had her head on Mama's lap, and we were positioned this way for about a minute when the van came to an abrupt stop, sending us flying towards the front and onto the dirty, smelly floor.

Someone unlocked the door and yelled "Let's go!" And in the light from the premises I noticed that it was a Black man. From then on, I tried to meet his eyes whenever I could, but he absolutely avoided my gaze. I wanted to make him feel guilty, I wanted to call him *mpimpi* and tell him he was only hurting his own people and no one else. It was not that I had never seen a Black policeman before, because I had many times. There were mostly Black policemen in the townships, but it was really the White ones who would be the leaders of the pack. But I think on that particular night, I was even more horrified by the presence a Black man in the police force. Because he had come so close to me, I really wanted to tell him exactly what I thought of him. I was frustrated and wanted someone to lash out at. It was not that I thought White policemen were entitled to being brutal, just that I was more afraid of them. It also made things more confusing for me, because I thought I understood where their hostility came from, and when I saw Black policemen it blurred my straight-cut analysis of who I had to watch out for. On that particular night, I wanted to take out my anger and fear on that one man who opened the door and yelled at us without even looking straight in our eyes.

I was about to be strongly reminded of my inability to face other people's shame when we walked into the police headquarters. There were so many women hugging their bodies, only half dressed the way we were, and men staring down at the floors. I remembered how I had felt when my mother had been held there for a night. I thought about how humiliated she had looked walking out of there and how I could not bare to look her in the eye, and I was suddenly apologetic for how I had felt at that time. The station was overflowing with people who had just been arrested, and it was clear that there had been police raids in many different townships. No one really stared at us the way I had anticipated, probably because they all had their own problems to worry about.

Our handcuffs were taken off and we were thrown in a stinky, filthy cell crowded with other women. I had no idea where to sit because it was so full in there. Keitumetse and I stayed close to Mama, who greeted a few women whom she had apparently worked with before. They exchanged stories about what had happened and one woman asked Mama about Keitumetse and Mohau, because her first thought was that we were being detained for our connection with him. I was a little taken aback by how well he was known all over the place. I knew people knew about him because the police had made no secret of being on the lookout for him, but I had no idea so many people had heard about him. But I was soon to discover that my underground work at the SASO was not as big a secret as I had always thought, either. Some people pointed to me as if they knew me from somewhere, and since I thought I had been so discreet, I was appalled.

As I stood there listening, my hand covering my nose from the stench, my eyes met those of a woman who looked about Keitumetse's age. She was standing in front of me, her straightened hair in a big mess and her eyes red like she had been crying for a long time. When I first saw her I got the feeling that she had been staring at me for a while, and for the first time since we first walked in, I felt self-conscious. But she stretched the tip of her lip on one side, giving me a tired smile, and said, "I've learned to sleep with my clothes on," and both of us gave off short, sad laughs.

"First night?" she asked, and I nodded.

"How long have you been in here?" I asked her in a husky voice and then cleared my throat.

"A day," she said, shrugging. I was stunned because I thought everyone had just come in from being dragged out of their homes in the middle of the night. My heart sank when I looked around at all those women's exhausted faces and imagined that my fear would soon turn into that same exhaustion and hopelessness. But I also noted that women of different ages were in there, and it gave me hope that I would be able to stay with my family.

In a few hours two police officers, a man and a woman, came in and called out the names of a few people, including me, Mama, and Keitumetse. *"Kom hier-so"* they yelled out to us, like they were calling out to disobedient animals. I clung to Mama with one hand and to Keitumetse with the other. To my surprise, my sister went before us, as if she was ready for whatever they had decided to do with her.

That was my first moment of extreme panic. I had no idea what they were about to do with us. One officer said to me, *"Klein kaffirs!* You're the worst ones," and told me to move fast if I didn't want his boot in my buttocks. He pushed me so hard that I let go of my sister's hand and she got lost in the shuffle as we hurried out to the room the female officer had pointed to. When we got in there, we saw that it was hardly big enough to hold a quarter of us, and they told other people to go into a different room. Mama was pulled and pushed into the other room, while I went into the first one.

It was bare with cold cement floors that looked every bit as filthy as the cell we had just come from. The policewoman who had called us out came in and put on a pair of gloves, and then took her baton and started hitting it threateningly against her palm. She told us to line up against the wall and face away from her. That was probably one of the most daunting commands, because it meant we had to turn away from whatever it was she had planned and she would have the power of doing whatever she wanted from behind us. We could not disobey her—most of us were too tired and some of us were too terrified of her. So we turned and pressed our faces against the wall. I thought I heard her leave and it was quiet for a while as we stood there powerless, awaiting our fate.

Minutes later she came back in. From the shuffling feet, it sounded like she was with a few other people, but only she spoke.

"Okay, women!" she yelled in Afrikaans. "Take off your clothes! Now!"

We shifted and turned around, hoping we had heard wrong. So she yelled it even harder, hitting her baton against a wall. "Now!" she said and we turned our backs to her and obeyed.

"Bend over, we're going to search you!" she yelled. My head began to hurt again and then it felt like it was spinning and I thought I could not move. My limbs felt numb, my hands shook. I managed to take a few steps back and arch my body forward, my head touching the wall. I turned to see what was going on and then I definitely could not move.

There were men with gloves on, opening women's buttocks wide and sticking their fingers in them. I was to learn that this was a common search routine. My head quickly turned back so that I hit the wall but, strangely, I felt no pain. I just stood there horrified, waiting my turn. Then someone whose face I never saw pulled my backside wide open and quite forcefully. It was as if he wanted to really stretch me wide enough so that he did not miss anything. His finger abruptly pushed in.

I began to count backwards from one hundred to distract myself until that stopped working, then I started remembering historical facts: Who was the first president of the ANC? Albert Luthuli . . . What year did South Africa get a new flag? 1902 . . . no, 1903 . . . no. Who was the first president of the Republic of South Africa?" I heard someone yell at me to get out of there already. When I left, there was no one else in that room.

*

We spent the night in a cell that was about the size of our tiny bathroom at home, with a backed-up toilet in the middle. There were six of us in the same cell with hardly any room to sleep. None of the women in there were people I had seen before, but I felt a lot safer with a group of Black people than I did with the policemen. I sat up and spent hours dozing in and out of sleep, my body shivering from the cold because I was still in my nightgown. I had many different dreams, and one kept coming back.

I dreamed that I was younger and I was playing with Thato on the street. We had just come home from school and had not gone home to change, but she was not in her school uniform. I kept asking her why she was wearing her own clothes and she just shrugged. In time I got really desperate, asking and asking why she was not in her school clothes. Finally she said, "Because I don't have to," and walked away. I kept waking up whimpering, which woke up one woman who slept next to me. Eventually she told me to put my head on her lap, calling me by my name even though I had no idea who she was.

The next day I kept asking people where my mother was, but no one seemed to know.

"We were pushed and shoved so many times last night, I'm sure even your mama has no idea how she got wherever she is," one woman told me.

There was sunlight coming in from the tiny window high above us in the cell. I had no idea which direction that window was facing, or what part of the building we were in, and neither did anyone else in that room. I was the youngest person in there and the women all took on the role of a caregiver to me. This was reassuring, but it was hard not to recognize them. I really needed to see Mama and Keitumetse. When it was time to eat, we went into a large cafeteria that smelled really awful and was filled with a lot of people. In there I tried to find my family but had no luck. The pain of being separated from them was excruciating and it was made worse by the fact that I hardly recognized anyone. I did not recognize the food they gave us to eat, and there were things crawling in it, so I refused to touch it.

At some point in the afternoon I was told that I was being moved to a different room, and I got excited because I thought that maybe I was being reunited with my family. Instead, I was moved into a room to be interrogated. A large policeman with very hairy arms pushed me onto a chair as soon as I walked in, saying he had been waiting a long time for me. I was about to cry, but I could not decide if that would give them more power or if it would make me seem too young and innocent to interrogate. In the end, I decided I could not be sure of anything, so I went with the option of forcing back my tears and taking very deep breaths to suppress the lump in my throat. The man with the very hairy arms stood sucking on a cigarette and blowing the smoke into my face, so that the room was so hazy with smoke I could not take deep breaths.

"Are you a *kommie*?" he yelled in my face. I tried to tell myself it would be like a quiz in order to feel less nervous, but that only worked a little bit. However, I had no idea what he was asking me, and only later found out *kommie* meant communist. To my surprise, I had never before heard how they said it in Afrikaans.

"No," I answered in the most polite voice I could manage.

"Listen here," he said in Afrikaans. "Don't waste my time here. You tell the truth, we let you go. End of story. Do you want to see your mom?" The mention of my mother made me break down.

"Yes," I sobbed and was about to say as much as I could just so they would let me see her, but I remembered what Mama had said in the van about them lying. I thought that it could not possibly get worse than that.

"Who have you been working with?" he asked me.

"No one," I said, and he leaned really close and slapped me really hard across the face. But instead of making me cry, the slap startled me.

He must have kept me in there for hours. I had no idea what time of day it was because there was no window in there, just artificial light. He just kept repeating himself over and over again, and in the middle of it I realized he had no idea who I was or what I had done, his job must have been to interrogate anyone who came in there. When he was not getting any satisfactory answers from me he said, "Do you know what electric shock is?" and I flinched just thinking about it, remembering the many stories I had heard from people who had been in detention.

"Yes." I answered, my voice quivering.

"So if you don't tell me about your *kommie* friends, you will be getting the electric shock very soon."

My head started pounding as he stood there staring me in the face. He walked out and then came back with a big box that he told me had "the equipment" in it. I was horrified, and on the verge of telling all about my work with the SASO, my friendship with Tshepo, and how I had cleared the office. I decided that if I said something about Mohau then he would let me go in a second. But I had to fight that impulse really, really hard. My will was weak and all I wanted was to see my mother. And he knew that, so he just kept pressing until I pretended to feel faint and he ordered that I be removed from that room until the next day.

But days went by before I was asked any questions again. I do not know how many days passed because I had no idea what was going on outside except for the light that came in through the window, letting me know it was daytime. At night I would hear women screaming from other cells, and I kept trying to see if I recognized their screams. My mind would wander at those times, because I was trying to decide how I could know my mother's screams if I had never heard her wail before. I would spend a lot of time pondering over really strange questions, just to remove myself from where I was. Almost every night now I slept on Ausi Joyce's lap—the woman who had offered her comfort to me on the first night. We were filthy, not having been allowed to wash ourselves because we had not disclosed any important information.

One day a policeman came to our cell and told me he had something for me. I was hopeful, thinking that maybe I would see my family. But in fact he took me to another interrogation room and told me to take off my clothes. I was horrified and afraid, but there were two of them, and they kept me in there for a long time, touching my breasts as they asked me questions. I was made to sit naked on a chair. I tried to cover myself with my arms, but one of them kept pulling my arms away from my chest so that he could have better access to my breasts. My feeling of being proud of my breasts, of liking how firm they were, was really hurt by that experience. That man's hands made me want to be out of my body, and I stopped enjoying the beauty of my body at that room. They had every name for my body except the words I used in my head.

"You look like a virgin, like you've never been touched. That's why those breasts are so firm, isn't it?" he said as he stood towering over me.

In my head stories of women being raped in jail kept coming and my headache would start and then stop again, then start again. It was strange how whenever I thought I was more horrified than I ever would be again, my fear level just kept rising. I kept crossing my legs and tightening the grip of my arms around my chest.

"You like growing up?" the other man asked me, and I just stared straight ahead of me, counting backwards: "200, 199, 198 . . ."

I tried to block out their sounds, but eventually they realized that they were not getting much of a reaction from me, and then one of them pulled my arms behind me while the other one fondled my breasts. Because my arms were being pulled so far back, my body was positioned in such a way that my chest protruded towards the man in front of me. In that way, if someone had walked in that room they would have thought I was giving him full permission to do whatever he wanted to do with me. I could not pull back my arms no matter how hard I tried, so I had to give that up. My biggest struggle now was to keep my legs tightly crossed. My mind went out and I was back in school, laughing at something Lebo said. And then I went from there to my home, where I was sleeping at my mother's side, clinging to her arm. I thought of Dikeledi and her voice, heard her speak about our struggle, our fight for safety and rights. I thought about Mama and Keitumetse and my whole body felt hot with rage. The man fondling my breasts suddenly pulled my legs apart. I had been using all the power in the world to keep them together and he parted them in just one swift move. No effort, just one simple, violent move. His pants fell to the floor just as quickly and he was not wearing anything underneath. I was petrified. I quickly realized that they would probably not want anyone out there to know what they were doing. I figured that they were allowed to hit me, but that this must be forbidden. My mind was racing, as I tried to think of what to do, how to discourage them before it was too late.

"Great!" I heard myself yell. "I'm so excited. I know it's illegal for me to sleep with a White man in this country, but if this is my lucky day, I may just consider breaking the law!"

The man fondling my breasts jumped back and the one behind me dropped my arms. I was just as startled as they were, but I was also furious, so I spoke louder.

"What are you going to do to me, huh?" I was hoping someone would hear my screams from the outside the way I had other women's cries. "Come on, I'm fourteen, but that's okay because I'm experienced and I'll be fifteen in a month if you're worried about age. You must be twenty-something, right? So that's not so bad. Officer Van Wyk?" I said his name because I had heard the other one call him that when they came in. I wanted someone outside to hear who was in here. If the other women could hear me, if these men hurt me more than they already had, then perhaps I would have witnesses. I kept yelling and yelling, telling them I knew exactly what kind of thing they were hoping for, and screaming their names over and over again. The one in front of me panicked and then started slapping, punching, and kicking me. I lay naked on the concrete floor, shrieking from the pain. But no one came in to see what was going on. It gave me an idea of what those other screams had been coming from, and I realized that there must have been some kind of policy allowing policemen to do whatever they wanted with the people they were interrogating. We were in the middle of a close-knit club of cruel and violent people who had to come and kick us out of our beds in the middle of the night and bring us to their mercy in cold dark rooms. They all knew what they were doing, and exactly what they had brought us here for. What they called our political activities was an excuse for these men to come and satisfy their own repugnant desires.

One of them told me to put my dress back on and pulled me by my arm, dragging me towards the door. My body scraped against the concrete floor, causing extreme pain. I thought the skin on my thighs would be torn. He dragged me all the way across the hallway, then he kicked my legs and demanded that I stand up. I managed to stand but had to arch my body because I was in so much agony. It was the kind of pain where after a while you start feeling nothing and your body becomes stiff. Eventually we reached a closed door in a dark passage, which he unlocked and threw me inside.

It was as if I had just flown into the night. There was absolutely no light in that cell. I assumed it was a small cell even though I had no idea where and how far apart the walls surrounding me were. It was extremely cold, even colder than the first cell I had been in. I did not see a window, so I knew that there was no way I would be getting sunlight. My feet were almost completely frozen, so I rubbed my hands together and then covered my toes with them. I spent most of my time in there rubbing warmth into my body. After hours of staring into the dark, I lay on my side and attempted to sleep, but it was just too cold. I had nothing to cover myself with, and it was simply impossible to fall asleep. So I stretched my hand out and started looking for a wall in the dark. There was a noise in the room, of things scurrying around. Then there they were, a pair of eyes, then another, and then another. I was so terrified, it took me no time at all to start shrieking again. The rats kept staring at me and then turned to go away for a while. I thought that the cell must be really big, because they had places to go and they looked like they were far enough from me. But in time they ran up towards me and one or two of them began gnawing at my feet.

I screamed at the top of my lungs but no one came. In time I realized that there was no way anyone could have heard me, considering the distance we had come from where all the other cells were. Furthermore, there was no opening except for the steel door that was tightly shut. I had to fight off the rats with my hands.

I would throw them hard and they would go flying and hit the floor a few feet away from me. It was excruciating. I cried and cried—for Mama, Keitumetse, my friends, everyone. When the rats were not biting me, they would run around, and I wondered if I would only be there for a few hours or if I would have to get used to them.

I thought it was morning after many long hours, because there were holes on one side of the room, across from what I thought was the wall, and light was seeping through them. My fear was fast reaching what was probably at its peak, and it finally turned into sheer exhaustion, the same fatigue I had seen on the faces of the women who had been in that large, overcrowded cell on our first night at the jail. I felt like I had spent the night doing incessant exercise. It was still freezing, and I kept putting my fingers in the holes in an attempt to warm them a little—one of the many senseless acts of desperation.

At one point in the day, a hole in the door opened and a hand pushed a plate through. I forgot to tell the hand that I at least needed something to cover myself with in the cold. The plate was again filled with something I could not name. I was so hungry that I had to eat, so I reached in and separated the slimy, foodlike stuff from the things that moved around the plate. Putting it in my mouth made me gag the first few times, but my stomach could not take the hunger anymore. I really needed the strength, so I just closed my eyes and counted backwards, imagining I was eating something I loved but that I had not eaten in a very long time. By the time I was finished and all that was left on the plate were the little crawling creatures, I had managed to convince myself that I had had a perfectly good meal.

I would have to get used to the cell—this was the punishment for refusing to satisfy a police officer's need to feel like a man. Maybe if I had been as good as they wanted me to be and not resisted, cursed, and screamed I would be in a cell with more light. I might even be resting on Ausi Joyce's lap. Maybe, I thought, they would have even let me see my mother and my sister. There was nothing to do in that cell, all day and all night I would sit there unable to sleep or stay awake. I was too tired to keep my eyes open and too afraid of the rats and my nightmares to sleep soundly. People I knew, friends and family, would come to my mind as I fell asleep against the wall, tired of warming my hands and feet.

Some nights I would be back in my childhood, playing with the little stones, telling stories of innocence. The mother rock would be kissing the father rock and there would be something warm about it but I would have no idea what that warm thing was between them. Whatever they would do together would be done with their consent. I was young and happy in those dreams, but they were brief, abruptly interrupted by the sound of a scurrying rodent coming for my leg.

Other nights I would be sitting there speaking to Tshepo. I had no idea sometimes if I was awake and speaking to myself, or if I was dreaming. In the dark it all started to feel the same. I would be climbing over a neighbour's fence to steal lemons, and all I cared about in the world was how yellow the lemons were. If they were green I would not take them, but Tshepo would. He would say that the sun would take care of it, you just had to pick as many lemons as you could carry in your arms. We would be stealing lemons not because we wanted to make lemonade or use them for flavour in our tea, but because of the thrill of climbing over someone's fence, stealing their fruit and escaping without getting caught. Sometimes even having someone yell out to you to stop making a mess in their yard was exciting and amusing. We could entertain ourselves really well on hot afternoons in the noisy township.

The hand kept coming and bringing me the plate with the noxious food. In time I became a pro at picking out and separating what was alive from what was just slimy but edible. Meanwhile, my bruises were not getting any better. I would sit there cold and in pain, some parts of my body feeling numb, and I would start imagining the peach trees. I had been there for so long that I had to think hard about what month we were in, but it had been spring when they put me in there, so I imagined and dreamed about the peach trees blooming. There is probably not a single rotten one, I thought. They are probably hard and green and not yet edible. In my mind I would go over and walk around the trees, impatiently feeling each peach, hoping to stumble upon one that was slightly ripe.

I thought about the fact that, if the peach trees were just beginning to bloom, it was probably around the time of Keitumetse's birthday. The dust had probably completely settled and the first rain must have come already. If, on the other hand, the fruit on the trees was turning from green to a slightly yellowish colour, then it would be closer to my birthday. The thought shocked me. I thought that I could already be fifteen and I would not know it. Maybe at this point, being unaware of what day or month it was, I could decide that I already was fifteen. Maybe. One reason I knew it had been a long time was that I had had my period twice already, although it seemed unusually short and light, and I had definitely missed about two since my last one. Whatever date it was, no one seemed to be coming for me. I was convinced that they had completely forgotten I was in the building, and that I had been left for dead. Except for the hand. The hand regularly brought me a plate and some water. Sometimes I would take the water and rub it against my armpits and my vagina—I had not had a bath since I had been in there and I felt unclean. When I first had my period in there I had yelled at the hand to bring me something to hold my blood, and it brought me a single rag that I bled through and then had to watch dry until the next time I needed it. So I used the little bit of water to clean myself, but I had to be careful about having enough to drink. The hand only brought one cup of water even if the plate came twice a day.

I had come to expect the hand and it appeared regularly, until one day when instead of the hand two large men opened the door and called me out. The light from the door was blinding and I did not get a good look at them. They yelled at me in Afrikaans to come out and I crawled towards them on my hands and knees, squinting. One of them pulled me up by the back of my nightgown and brought me to my feet. Then he pulled me by my arm all the way until we were back in the part of the building where I had been the first few days. All that way he walked quickly, dragging me along so that I tried to keep up but it seemed almost impossible. All the while he cursed and yelled at me for looking "*vyl,*" or filthy. Not being able to fully open my eyes only made it worse. I felt that I had to be as quick as possible, thinking it would make him stop cursing, but he just kept on yelling out insults.

Finally, we went into an interrogation room and he pushed me onto a chair. I put my hands over my eyes for a minute and parted my fingers so that it was like I was looking through the holes in my cell that brought light through the wall. Slowly I was able to open my eyes more, but it was still really difficult.

"We are letting you go," one of the men said in Afrikaans. "You just have to tell us who you were working with. Tell us who organized that march and you can go home"

I sat in silence, unsure of what would satisfy them.

"I have no idea, I just marched with the crowd," I said.

He hit his hand against the armrest of the chair I was sitting on, and then put his face really close to mine. I could smell cigarettes on his breath and it made me nauseous, so I turned my head away from him.

"Listen to me! I've had it with your little *kaffir* lies. You give me some answers and stop wasting my time!" His voice got louder as he got angrier. He just stood back and the two of us stared at each other for what seemed like ages.

"Fine!" he said. "Andries!" he called out to the other policeman who had not said a word to me, and who I had not really looked at until that minute. I wondered if he was the same man who had opened the back of the van for me and my family on that first night, but I could not be sure. "Get the electric shock!" He said the words "electric shock" in English, his "r" sounding like a roar. The man called Andries went out for about ten seconds and came back with a box full of equipment. I was not as terrified as I would have been when I first got to detention. I just took one look at the box with its wires and the shocks and gave in before they ever touched my body. The man in charge started to shock my body. First my breasts, then my back. It burned like nothing I had ever felt before. He kept asking questions but I could not hear anything, I thought I was going to die. I was sure I was going to die.

Then he told the man called Andries to take me out and give me a bath, because I smelled so bad. "You *kaffirs* never know how to take care of yourselves. Your mother never taught you to wash?" he kept saying, over and over again.

Andries dragged me again through some hallways, but this time I could not feel the pain of my body scraping against the concrete floor. The burns were unbearable. When we finally reached a musty room with a small filthy bath in it, he filled it and threw me in the cold water. I was sure that I was dying. I kept thinking, I will never see my family again, I will never get out of here alive. After a few minutes in the cold bath with my gown on, he told me to get out and follow him. He brought me back to the interrogation room, where I had to take my clothes off and wait to dry. While I was drying the other man slapped, kicked, and hit me with his baton. Once I was dry he resumed the shocking.

"See what happens to little *kaffirs* who don't obey the law?" he said.

I did not know if I was conscious or not. My neck bent far forwards and my chin was resting on my chest. Then I started to vomit. I had never vomited before and was shocked by how violent the whole act was. I spewed the slimy things I had been eating all over the floor. One of the men picked me up by my arm and dragged me through the vomit and out the door.

I was back in the bath, sure that I would die any second. Soon I was back in a cell, alone. This time it was brighter because there was a window above me. I just lay there on the cold concrete floor, seeing and speaking to people I now knew only in my dreams. Sometimes it was my mother telling me stories, other times I was younger and playing on the streets, running and running. I would be talking about becoming a journalist or I would be at the SASO office at the typewriter, writing for the newsletter. Most of the time I would be running around in the streets, playing and never getting tired. They say I was in that cell for a month and in the jail for six months. This is what they tell me, I could not tell you myself. I was fifteen years old plus a few months when I was released.

In the hospital I lay on the bed facing the ceiling, grateful for the warmth of the flimsy sheets on top of me. I was so badly hurt that for days I had no idea where I was. Mama said that it was as if I was out of my body, because it looked limp, like I had no control over it. My family came every day, at every visiting hour. Mama was now working up on the hill for a Black family in the township. She had lost her job after not being there for weeks because she was in detention. My sister was released only a few days after we went in, they say she cried so much that the police simply had no patience for her. Mama was tortured for weeks before they let her go, and she said they let her go only because she kept begging them to release me and keep her. Knowing that it would have been extremely painful for her to go and leave her child there, they let her go.

I missed the mass funeral of the comrades who died in the massacre because of having been in detention. My family comes to tell me what is going on in the outside world. I feel really cut off and I long for contact with familiar faces. It is February, they tell me, and it is a new school year. Just about everyone I know is repeating standard eight because of the riots and not getting to study or learn enough in school the previous year. My sister tells me who the funeral was for: Peter, Thabang, Dikeledi, and a lot of people I worked with at the SASO. I recognize most of the names but cannot always recall everyone's voices or faces, which is just as well because it is always hard to dream about the ones I remember well. I prefer to just know their names. Lebo is apparently now in a different school. A lot of people change schools in the hopes of finding teachers who are not too exhausted or too afraid to walk into a class and teach. The chances of them finding teachers like that in the township are slim, but they keep hoping and moving.

My sister and my mother do not tell me about their experiences in jail, and I do not tell them about mine. We are too afraid to know about each other's experiences, especially since we are still in shock over our own torment. Both of them look gaunt and tired, but Mama

Kagiso Molope

is happy about not having to take the train to work anymore and being able to work so close to home. "It saves time and money," she tells me—and that is the only thing she says about herself. My sister does not say a lot about herself either, she has not even mentioned Mohau or Tshepo in the time that she and my mother have been coming to see me. If I want to know about Mama I have to ask Keitumetse and if I want to know about Keitumetse I have to ask Mama. I have an unspoken agreement with both of them: I will not speak with either one of them directly about their well-being, but they each know that I will ask the other. This is their time to take care of me, and they say things like "You just rest" and "Don't worry about us," but I know their experiences were traumatic and that they are still in shock. All three of us turn our experiences into private, intimate matters that are meant only for our hearts. If we ever speak about it, it will probably be about the cursing and the beatings, not about the other things—the more humiliating ones that involved us being naked. The ones that could only have happened to us because we are women. Those stories are a source of shame. We will keep them to ourselves until we understand that we were assaulted by men who were afraid of our will. Our suffering gave a sense of worth to men who would probably not be able to wake up in the morning or look themselves in the mirror if they thought for a second that they could do nothing about our feelings of entitlement to what belongs to us. If they thought that we were not afraid of them, they would never be able to live with themselves. But for now we do not know that and if we do we cannot fully understand it, because all we carry is the shame. We are not aware of their fear, so we can only feel the humiliation they forced upon us. So we all pretend that there is not much more to tell each other, and we go on and on doing this for so long that after a while I begin to think we are almost convinced this is the whole truth.

In the night, when visiting hours are over and everyone is gone, I lie in my bed grateful that the lights are off and I cannot see the cockroaches on the walls and floor. I cringe when I think that they may crawl over me in my sleep. But after a few nights in the hospital I know that cannot sleep because I might dream of men in uniform, whose faces have replaced those of my fellow comrades in my dreams. I think of places I have never been to, places I will go when I walk out of the hospital. I wonder about school—whether or not I can walk into class close to the middle of the year and still be able to know what was going on. I am smart, I think to myself, I knew more than most of the people in my class just before the police took me. I'm sure we could probably be on about the same level when I return. I want to go back, I would like to pretend that life can go on and that we can recover from everything that has happened.

A figure arrives in the dark, and I am afraid because I have no idea what is going on. I wonder if I am awake or dreaming. I was sure that I was awake. I shake my head and attempt to escape from the dream, but nothing happens, the figure remains in front of me.

"Who are you?" I ask.

She leans over so that I can see her face, and I am startled. I almost scream, but decide I am not afraid of her. I stare back at her to alleviate the nervousness.

"Shhh," she whispers. "Lie back and rest. Let me tell you a story."

"About what?" I ask her.

"About someone you know," she says, and then she sits down and begins.

"Setshiro left his family many many years ago on a train headed for Gauteng. He was going to find ways to feed his family, take care of his little sister and his parents. His intention was to work in the mines like most men, and he thought that was probably his only option. So he left with all the hope in the world. But when he arrived in Gauteng, it was not as simple as he had hoped. He had his pass but could not find anything in the mines for the first little while.

"One day a friend told him that he knew someone who was looking for a gardener, so he went there and asked to see the owner of the house. At the end of that day Setshiro had his first job in the City of Gold. It did not involve digging for gold underground, and it paid less than he had anticipated, but he took it anyway. He worked there every day, tending to a White man's garden, and they said he was a good worker. They named him Tobias because they had no patience for a Setswana name, and all in all it was a good job and he had money to send home. Everything was perfect. Until he fell in love with Diana.

"Some say Diana was a rebellious teenager with liberal ideas who wanted to upset her parents, but others say she fell in love with a man the way any girl falls in love at her age, and there was nothing more to it. Setshiro wrote letters to his sister at home telling her about Diana, the love of his life. He wanted Diana and his sister to meet, the two women he cared about most in his life, but they never did. All his sister ever knew about Diana was what she read in her brother's letters.

"One day, Diana told Setshiro that she was going to have a child. He panicked and was afraid of being arrested because falling in love with a woman of a different colour was against the law. And sure enough, when her parents found out, Setshiro was put in jail, accused of raping his boss's daughter. Some say Diana defended her lover as much as she could, others say that she was quiet and obedient and never said a word in his defence. Either way, she was never to see him again, and her parents made sure of it. She also refused to get rid of the child, which infuriated her father even more. So they decided that as embarrassing as it was, she would go away and have the baby, but that she would have to give it away because they were afraid of their family and friends knowing finding out what was going on. In the meantime, Diana wrote letters to her lover's sister about her love for the man she called Tobias and the child she was about to have. Setshiro's sister went to the City of Gold to find the house of Diana's parents, and when she did, she pleaded with them to let her raise her brother's child. Her father was only too pleased to give the child away, and her mother could really not have cared less what they did with that baby, as long as it was out of her house.

"They say that when the day came, Diana didn't even have a minute with her child. She gave birth at the home of one of her mother's sisters, somewhere far away in the rural areas. Setshiro's sister was called on that very same day to come and take the child away. Diana's mother never even looked at the baby, while the father is said to have been sad to let her go. Setshiro's sister raised her as her own, just as she had raised her first child."

There is silence between us after she tells me. Both of us stare at nothing in particular, unable to see each other's faces clearly in the darkness. All we hear are people's coughs and cries from pain in the hospital ward. The cockroaches are scratching, scurrying across the wall above my head.

"What happened to Setshiro?" I ask.

"The police say he committed suicide in jail."

"Oh," I say, my heart beating harder and harder.

For the first time in many months, I fall asleep and dream of things I have never dreamed of before: Ships and planes. The Drakensberg mountain. The Andes. The Rockies. The Himalayas. Kilimanjaro. I see mountains and oceans over and over again. Beautiful things and places I have never laid my eyes on before. Places I have only read about. Mma Kleintjie left sometime after she told her story, and in the dark I could feel her relief at getting it all off her chest.

When I return home, the township looks and feels like home. Except I know there are so many people missing. There are students in their black and white school uniforms walking the streets when you know they should be in school. They probably have tired and depressed teachers sitting in staff rooms, waiting for something to go wrong. I am so relieved to be home that it feels a little bit overwhelming. The first thing I want do is take a warm bath. I want to sit in there and soak like Mama sometimes does at the end of a long day, but I think of the bath in jail and my head feels dizzy and I cannot bring myself to slip into the bathtub. I decide to take the small round bowl that we use for doing the washing, and I fill it up with warm water. Although this is not as satisfying, there is more water in it than I have seen for months, and I am bathing in the privacy of my home. After this I am surprised because I still feel unclean. I stand and stare at the water, throw it out and fill up the bowl one more time and begin to bathe all over again as if I am doing it for the first time. I scrub and scrub as hard as I can, but I still feel dirty. For hours in the afternoon I keep doing this. Sometimes I go as far as getting dressed and then taking off my clothes and starting from the beginning.

After a while I force myself to go and sit outside. I am excited to see Mama come home before dark and realize it will be the first time in my life I've seen her do so. The first time that she will be home hours before it is time to sleep. So I sit and wait on the front *stoep* and look out onto the street, watching children laughing and running around trying to kick a ball. They have two bricks on either side of the road and they kick the ball towards the bricks. Every time a car comes they run to get off the road, and then they resume their game. I look over at Tshepo and Mohau's house and get a really heavy feeling in my chest. I still have no idea what country they are in, and Mama said Keitumetse have not said anything about them in months. Mohau's aunts are supposed to have moved, they decided to go to live with relatives in another township.

When Mama comes, she gives me a broad smile and sits next to me. Her knees are very dark from kneeling and scrubbing another woman's floors all day, and she looks tired, but not too much.

"Did you eat?" she asks me.

"Yes," I lie.

She starts to tell me about her new job. Her boss is a nice woman who is a lawyer just like her husband. They have two children who are in the same school as Thato. I ask her how Thato is, and she shrugs. I don't think I really want to know that badly anyway, so I let her finish telling me about the large house owned by the people she works for. After she stops I take a deep breath and hug my body.

"Mama?"

"Hmmm?" she says.

"Where is Diana now?"

She too hugs her body and does not look at me for a few minutes. She just sits staring at the children playing on the street, not really taking in anything they are doing. Then she gets up and leaves.

"I'm going to cook supper," she informs me. I just sit staring at the children playing, wondering what she is going to do with my question.

If she is angry I am not afraid, I think to myself. The children cheer, someone has just scored a goal.

In the morning, before she goes to work, my mother gives me a telephone number with Diana's name on it. I wait until Keitumetse is out of the house and gone to see the neighbours before I dial it. My hands are shaking, but I am not so afraid and I feel ready to dial the number. On the other side, an elderly woman answers. I would like to fake an English accent but it is impossible, I do not feel that confident. I tell her I am an old friend of Diana and ask if she is there. She says no, Diana is in Canada, and she is not coming back. I ask when she left and, without realizing that I must have told a lie by calling myself an old friend, she says "years ago," and there is a long pause between us.

I am trying to speak kindly and fluently in a language that I have come to associate only with punishment. So I have to take deep breaths before I speak. I can hear that the woman on the other side is impatient but does not say a word.

"Can I have her telephone number?" I ask politely.

"Wait," she says, and I can hear her put down the phone, her footsteps moving away from my ear. Eventually they come back and her voice sounds softer this time.

"I can give you her address. She is travelling right now so I know she doesn't have a phone."

"Thank you," I say after she reads the number to me. "How is she?"

"Fine, I think. She doesn't call or write much. I think she is happy, she just travels a lot."

"Has she been back to South Africa lately?"

"No," she says, and then pauses awhile so that I feel really regretful about having asked her. "She doesn't like to. Who are you again?"

"We are old friends." I don't want to lie any more than I have to because I may not be able to answer more of her questions.

"Hmmm. Well, did you used to be the neighbour's girl? I know she used to be friends with the neighbour's girl. She always liked them."

"No. But thank you." I hang up, angry with the woman for calling me a "girl" just because of my accent. But I do not want to resent her too much, so I think of how I am happy that she finally did give me Diana's address, even though I have no idea why I wanted it.

Mama refuses to speak to me about Diana. My need to not upset her takes over and I think it is best for me to not ask any more questions, and I will not go to Mma Kleintjie to ask anything either. So I ask Keitumetse, of course.

"Have you ever heard of Diana?" I ask her.

"No. Who is that?"

"I think someone Mama used to know, a long time ago."

Keitumetse looks puzzled.

"What do you know about her?" she asks. For a minute I have no idea how to put it and I pause before I say anything.

"She is the woman who gave birth to me," I say.

Keitumetse looks surprised, but less than I had expected. She says, "What woman?"

"I heard this. Don't ask me how, but Mama is angry that I found out."

"Oh!" my sister says. "The woman, the child."

"What?" I wrinkle my forehead and narrow my eyes.

"They used to say—"

"Who used to say?"

"The women. Mama and Ausi Martha and everyone. They used to say, 'That child had no idea what she would do with a Black baby.' They used to say that."

"What?" I am shocked that she never mentioned this to me either.

"I remember hearing about this child who had a child. I thought about this a lot when I was pregnant. I remembered that when I was little, the women used to talk a lot about this 'child' being a mother too soon in her life." So everything begins to make sense, and it becomes clearer and clearer that it is best not to discuss it with Mama.

As time goes on I am unsure of what to do. I do not know if I really want to know her, but I do think that I want her to know me. For some reason I feel sorry for her. Based on the little information I have, I already feel sad for this young woman who had a child that she never met, and who is now alone somewhere in the world, finding it hard to communicate with her parents.

The day after speaking to Keitumetse, I decide to go and speak to Ausi Martha. I am uncomfortable leaving the house because I feel self-conscious, uneasy with my own body. Every step I take, I feel as if all eyes in the neighbourhood are on me. For the first time in my life I think they stare with disgust instead of the love and concern I have always known from them. In my mind I hear them say the kinds of things that they would not want to say to my face. When I greet them, I cannot look them in the eye. I cannot even ask how they are. I feel their gaze on the dirt on my skin. They focus on my behind, my too-large breasts. They know everything, I think to myself, my feet not taking me fast enough on that short distance from my house to Ausi Martha's. In the back of my head I know very well that this is the voice of shame speaking, making me think that I am less of a woman because of things that happened to me—things that make me want to not be inside my own body.

Ausi Martha is standing, hanging the washing on the clothesline. When she notices me walk through her gate she drops everything and comes running and yelling.

"*Iyoo!!* Tihelo! Tihelo!"

My arms are hugging my body. I tighten my fists and raise my shoulders. I have no idea what to say, I am so touched by her being so happy to see me, and it makes me feel as if she does not see the rest of me—something I am grateful for. She just rushes and wraps her whole body around me, kissing me repeatedly on my lips, my cheeks, and my forehead. She is elated. Ausi Martha has always been a big woman but today I feel a lot smaller next to her because I lost so much weight in the past few months.

"*Iyoo*, Tihelo! *Iyoo, ngwanake*, my child! She keeps saying this, over and over again.

She puts my face in her hands and takes a long look at me, her eyes so loving and so sad. I know without her saying it that she thought she would never see me again. She wipes her watering eyes and says, "*Sho!*" As if to tell me she really has no words for me.

"Come and drink some cold drink," she offers. We walk towards the tree and sit in the shade, and she yells out to a child on the street to come over and take some money and a bottle so that he can buy us Sprite at Karabo's tuck shop. When the child comes over he looks at me curiously. I think that he must have heard about my ordeal and I look away to avoid his gaze.

"*Wena*, I can't believe it! I didn't want to come and see you. I heard you were back, but I didn't want to come see you until I heard you were a little bit better."

"Actually, I'm fine. I am a lot better." I lie and she pretends to believe me. I think that people have a harder time facing women from detention because they are afraid to look into your eyes and have all kinds of questions, specifically about sexual assault, and they feel that they cannot ask you because it is too embarrassing both for you and for them. It is strange how people can feel sorry for you when you have been beaten, but ashamed for you when they think you have been sexually assaulted.

The child-whose-name-I-don't-know comes back with a litre of Sprite and Ausi Martha thanks him by giving him five cents for a flavoured ice-pop. Before the boy leaves Ausi Martha sends him to get us some glasses to drink with. Without wasting too much time, I go straight to what I came for.

"I know about Diana," I announce.

Ausi Martha is shocked and asks me how I know, so I lie and tell her Mama told me.

"Ha!" she exclaims with surprise.

"She told me in the hospital. She was very sad to tell me, but said she thought that I should know now." Ausi Martha takes a sip of her Sprite, and spills everything so fast, I know I've succeeded in making her think that she has permission from Mama to talk.

She tells me that when Mma Kleintjie first came to the township, she took a special interest in me because of my light skin. She befriended Mama because she wanted to be close to me. No one thought anything of it, they just said it was probably because I was the only other person in the location with skin as light as hers. Maybe I looked like someone in her family, they thought. But then one night she revealed to Mama that she had been unhappy for so long because her own child had been taken away from her. The Group Areas Act, the Immorality Act, and the Mixed Marriages Act all came together and worked against her. She had broken all three laws because she had married a White man, had a child with him, and lived with them both. When they were discovered, the government declared that they were not supposed to be married or live in the same area.

Her child looked White according to the government officials, and so they had to be separated. Because she looked Coloured, she was the one who had to move away from the White area and far from her family.

"They looked at everything, her hair, her nails, everything," Ausi Martha tells me. "She had to move. She told your mother that she never saw them again because her husband suddenly turned into the most law-abiding citizen in South Africa. He was not willing to fight it."

"How old was the child?"

"I think she was about your age. Anyway, she kept insisting that Kgomotso tell you because every child deserves to know her mother. But your mother refused, she didn't want you to think that only Keitumetse was her child. She wanted both of you to feel as if you both belonged to her."

I am stunned. "How many people know?" I ask Ausi Martha, who by now has drunk most of the Sprite while I have not had much of it.

"Everyone."

"So no one told me?"

"No. No one would take a Coloured woman's position against that of your mother. You know that."

And I do.

I walk around the house preoccupied with this for days, unable to make up my mind about what I want to do. Over time I begin to reflect on what I have done with the SASO, what I have spent the past year doing with my life. I want to talk about it, tell it all to someone else. One day Mama hands me back the tapes and books that I brought home from the office, and I spend days listening and reading, remembering my comrades and everything we did together. When I hear Miriam Makeba and Letta Mbuli's pleading voices over the headphones, I feel like I am in good company. They sing about children, schoolchildren, a lot. Miriam Makeba sings about the township, sending our cries out into the world, refusing to be silenced. "*Khauleza*, hurry up, run," she keeps saying to us. She sings of students running away from the police, of dodging bullets and feeling afraid and confused. It becomes easier to take pride in what we did when I remember the days of being at the headquarters and the spirit of revolution. I think of Dikeledi a lot. I allow myself to hear her voice and listen to her speak. I let myself see her laugh, see the lines around her mouth, the brightness of her eyes, the strength in her face. I allow myself to grieve for a while, letting some things go and holding on to others. There is a lot of power in some of the memories. It is my life and cannot can be denied. All my experiences and everyone I have known will be with me wherever I go. Considering that the struggle is not over, I will need to take the faces of my friends wherever I go. I will need to remember what they stood for and what they died for in order to keep going, until we achieve the freedom we are fighting for. Until, hopefully, I see Tshepo and Mohau again.

So one night as I lie in bed, trying to think of ways to be in touch with Diana, I decide to write her a letter, one that I may never post, but one that I really need to compose.

Dear Diana,

I know virtually nothing about you, and I believe you know nothing about me either. I think that we have never met, or at least that was what I understood from a story told to me by someone who seems to know a lot about my history. I am the child you had fifteen years ago and never even got to see. The reason I do not introduce myself by the name I have been called all my life is because it is probably a name you do not know. You may have something else that you call me, if you think of me often enough. I thought I would write you a letter telling you a little bit about myself in the hope that you will someday write and tell me a little about yourself.

I have been with my mother, Kgomotso, since the day your father gave me to her. I have a sister, Keitumetse, and neither of them look anything like me, which is something I have always been curious about until the one night in the hospital when I heard about you and it all began to make sense. I have lived in the township all my life. Everyone I have ever loved is here. Well, many are gone now for reasons beyond our control, but some are still here. I do not know what you see on television there in Canada, I don't even know what you have read in the newspapers, but I will tell you a little bit about my life.

I almost lost my sister months ago because she was pregnant but did not want to have the child, and she terminated the pregnancy. Actually, I helped her do that because, you see, I don't know how you worked your life out after you had me, but here where we live a young woman's life cannot really go on as she wishes after she has had a child. I thought we had to prevent that from happening, so I got some medicine from a friend and gave it to my sister to drink, but she ended up in hospital and was very sick for a while. I was really scared, but she recovered and was back home shortly after that.

Then later I marched with a whole group of comrades because so many of our neighbours and friends had been taken into detention, but *many comrades ended up killed in a massive bloodbath. I lost a lot of friends there, but I missed their funerals because I was detained a few days after the massacre. I imagine you've seen South African riots on television there in Canada and you probably wonder what on earth we think we were doing throwing stones at men with large, deadly rifles. Well, we were trying to be listened to, that's all. But we do not have a voice here, on our streets or the streets your parents live on. Nor do we have a voice in government because we do not get to decide who rules us and who doesn't, because, as you must know, we do not have the right to vote. My mother is well into her thirties but she has never voted in her life. I am sure if you lived here you would have that privilege. I think it is strange that the woman who gave birth to me may know what that feels like while I, her child, may never know.*

You must have heard about all of this before, and the only reason I am telling you is because it is what I live, and I want to share with you who I am, because you never knew me. In time I plan to be a journalist. What do you do, Diana? What part of Canada do you live in? I heard from the woman who answered the phone at your parents' house that you travel a lot. I cannot imagine that amount of freedom, just being able to decide where I go and not having to stay within this area all the time. The thought of it is exhilarating. I have never even seen much of South Africa, except the township and town. But I do think about where I have not been a lot. I imagine what may be out there all the time. Since I heard you were in Canada I think about that country too. Do people have passes in Canada? I read that there are people called natives, the way we are also called here, and I also know that they live in places called reservations that are separate from the White people. What are the reservations like? Are they like townships? Have you ever been to a township? Because if you have, I'm sure you have made the comparison.

Are you happy there? I hope so. I am not happy here, but I am close to family, and that is comforting. I look forward to hearing about you and your life in that faraway land. Or, if you ever come to South Africa, maybe we can meet. Maybe we can meet somewhere where it is permissi-

ble for us to sit at the same table, face each other, and talk. If you come to South Africa and if you want to meet, I hope there will be such a place, because I would really like to hear about you and your travels. It would be really interesting too to hear the story of my birth. Well, until next time.

If you are ever looking for me in South Africa, my name is Tihelo Masimo, Revolutionary.

Acknowledgments

Mama Lali, Mama Meisie, Mama Gloria. My sisters, Choarelo, Tumelo and Lopang. Malome Aubrey, Malome Tiego, Thabang, Tshiamo, Ditshwanelo le Bolerileng, ke le rata thata thata thata! Nurjehan Aziz for believing in my work and treating it with so much care. Myma for being there since the beginning. Jacob for friendship, Benj and Dan for being my brothers. Special thanks to Jen Chang for unrelenting support and encouragement; a Peach Tree to Darryl Le Roux for all the hours we spent on the phone and for not telling me about the time difference! And my most righteous partner Jen, for staying up to read it and for loving me so fearlessly.

Peace and Power to you all,
Kagiso